The Unmarked Grave

A True Story of Romance, Love, Faith, Deceit and Tragedy

WRITTEN AND ILLUSTRATED BY
HASKELL A. DAVIS

First Printing: 2013

ISBN 13: 9780615886466
ISBN 10: 0615886469
LCCN: 2013916846
Haskell A. Davis, North Carolina

Glenwood Publishing Company
2120 Old Hwy 221 South
Marion, NC 28752

Special discounts are available on quantity purchases by associations, educators, and others. For details contact the publisher at the above address.
US trade bookstores and wholesalers: please contact Glenwood Publishing Company:
828-738-3524 or Haskell.davis@morrisbb.net.

Dedicated to **James Calvin Byrd**, *who inspired the writing of this book.*

Contents

Foreword ·vii

Acknowledgments · ix

Introduction· xi

Chapter One ·1

Chapter Two ·13

Chapter Three ·33

Chapter Four ·45

Chapter Five· ·61

Chapter Six ·71

Chapter Seven ·83

Chapter Eight· ·89

Chapter Nine · 105

Chapter Ten· 111

Chapter Eleven· 129

Chapter Twelve · 137

Chapter Thirteen · 153

Appendix · 161

Bibliography· 175

Foreword

"For jealousy is the rage of man: therefore he will not spare in the day of vengeance" (Proverbs 6:34).

Dotting the mountains of Western North Carolina are the rapidly disappearing ruins of old, fallen log homes. Each has its own story to tell, but in most cases, when the residents of these cabins have moved on, the tales have been lost forever.

These vine-covered structures represent history itself in their stately rockwork and logs so painstakingly hewn and fit in order to keep out the harsh elements. They are an enduring testimony to the rugged mountain men and women who left them behind. If we knew the stories of these log homes, we would have a better appreciation of the past, but sadly most today leave us with many unanswered questions.

This story takes place in one of these log houses with a beautiful and remote backdrop. When the author visited the house of Charlie and Frankie Stuart Silver in1966, it had already fallen down. The logs were decaying more with each passing day, and only half of the stately chimney still stood.

But while standing amid the fallen logs and gazing into the handsome remainder of the fireplace, I wondered what tale this place could tell of it colorful past.

This story follows the lives of Charlie and Frankie, real people, along with their families and members of their community. It tells the tragedy that changed their lives forever, although, like many legends, their tale of deceit, misunderstanding, and violence has been told in so many different ways much of the truth is distorted or no longer known. The author has therefore taken the liberty of choosing what he thought might best tell the story.

My purpose in writing this is to reveal the simple fact that the decisions we make in a moment can affect many lives right down through the ages. Our decisions should never be made in haste and without counting the costs. What takes place in this story contains lessons that should never be forgotten.

Acknowledgments

A very special acknowledgment must be made of **James Calvin Byrd** of Green Mountain and Burnsville, North Carolina. One night in our dorm room at Montreat-Anderson College in 1963, James Byrd related this story to me and a group of our friends. We sat spellbound as he told us what had happened years ago near where he grew up in Green Mountain. I could not get this story out of my mind. I asked him to take me to the place where it had happened.

One Sunday afternoon, also in 1963, after attending chapel, we loaded a group of our friends into my dad's old Rambler station wagon and made our way to Kona or Deyton's Bend. We parked and went through a cow-pasture gate and up a little road, and there we found a pile of decaying logs with a beautiful fireplace and chimney still standing. It was a sobering sight. With this my interest was heightened even more.

I decided to get information from some articles in old newspapers and books I found. J. Byrd told me he knew where the grave of Frankie Silver was located. He said he would help me find it. One Saturday in the winter of 1963, while still attending Montreat, we headed to Morganton to find the grave and the location of the old Buckhorn Tavern. When we located the site, I found myself completely immersed in this tragic story. While standing there gazing at the head stone of Frankie Silver, I turned to J. Byrd and said, "Someday I'll write about this." We took several pictures with an old camera I had there.

I started writing this story while I was at Montreat. I had three chapters written and then put it away. After *forty-seven years* I found my three chapters in a box tucked away in the basement. Then I decided to fulfill my promise to my former college roommate.

Thanks to **William George Silver, Jr.**, who has collected information about Charlie Silver and Frankie Stuart and helped set up a museum in the little Kona Baptist Church. He shared information and took me on a tour of the area. I wish to thank him for answering my questions and for his hospitality.

Thanks also to **Wayne Silver** for helping me locate the old Silver Cemetery.

To my wife, **Wilma Boone Davis**, thank you for your assistance and support. Without your help and patience, I never would have completed this dream.

Introduction

In a small, inconspicuous area called Kona, the children of George Silver, Jr. found their home among the steep mountain slopes of what is today Mitchell County, North Carolina. This region was originally part of Burke County.

When George, Sr., who had emigrated from Germany in the 1750s, was serving in the Revolutionary War, he passed through this area. He served under General George Washington. When he was no longer able to serve, George, Jr. served in his place. George, Jr. returned to these mountains with his son, Jacob, to stake out a land grant, dated 1819, make a home there, and spend the rest of his life in the beautiful mountain wilderness.

The Blue Ridge Mountains formed a barrier to the south of the Silver home. The majestic Roan Mountain stood as the boundary to the northeast. The group of Great Smoky Mountains formed another partition farther to the northwest. Also to the southwest were the beautiful and stately Black Mountains, one of which would later be named Mount Mitchell. Here, for millions of years, a strong and powerful stream—the Toe River, from the Indian name "Estatoe"—helped carve out these majestic mountains and valleys.

This story takes place where the North Toe and the South Toe Rivers merge. Here generations of the well-respected Silver family eked out their living and called this mountainous valley home. They play a significant part in the story that follows.

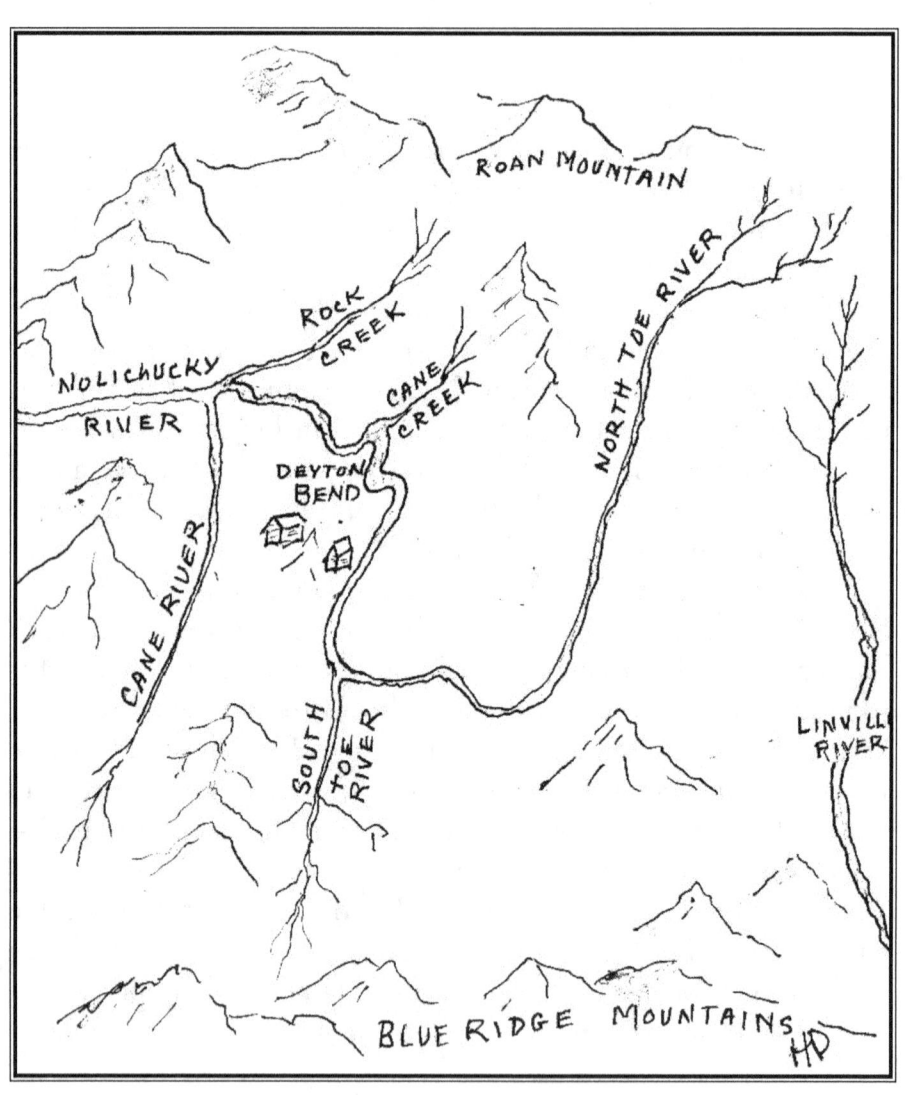

Chapter One

The cold wind pushed leaves across the valley floor with a steady moan. Occasionally the full moon broke through the clouds, casting eerie shadows. Charlie Silver had been awakened by a steady tap, tap upon the rickety, failing upstairs window. He went to it to find a tiny limb of the gigantic oak, encouraged by the wind, tapping on the window. He had almost hopped back into bed again when a distant screech caught his ear.

Charlie whispered, "Al, wake up. There is something outside!"

Al, his younger brother, did not respond. He was fast asleep on the straw tick covered with thick, heavy quilts.

Going closer to the window, Charlie saw an owl flutter away in the distance. Suddenly he froze as the moon broke through again. High on the hill above their log home, in the Silver family burial plot, stood what appeared to be a silhouette of a person. The moon disappeared again, leaving Charlie to wonder what he had seen, if anything at all.

Was it a grave marker, or was this just a dream?

Charlie Silver was twelve years old and a truly brave boy for his age. His dad, Jacob Silver, was a preacher and had fought in the Mexican War. Jacob, with the help of his father, George, had created a large, two-story log home in Kona, down in the valley below the Kona Baptist Church. Jacob had moved there with his second wife, Nancy Reed, after his first wife had died giving birth to Charlie. Soon Charlie would have many brothers and sisters. There was four years' difference between him and his brother Alfred.

"Al, wake up. There is something going on out there."

There was still no response from Al.

Charlie was freezing. He reached back to the bed, pulled a quilt from it, and returned to the window. The quilt felt good around his shoulders. He wondered if he should go wake his mom and dad.

The wind still howled nervously outside, encouraging the steady tapping on the small window. The moon came out from behind the clouds. He soon realized that what he saw was not a dream or his imagination because this figure was slowly making its way down the hill from the cemetery. Charlie started shaking, and the quilt could do little to warm him now. His feet were frozen, and his teeth were chattering.

While the figure continued to move, the moon became much brighter. The figure reached the main road and continued to move slowly and deliberately. It reached the roadway leading to Charlie's home and paused, then slowly began making its way through the yard.

Charlie could see it was a man. He had a strange load in his arms. The bright moonlight almost glistened as it struck the dark bundle the man was carrying. The snow and leaves rushed past him as if to get out of his way.

Paw Paw had told Charlie many stories by the fireside of ghosts and goblins. But this was far scarier, and Charlie could hardly breathe. Would he have time to go wake his mom and dad?

He pressed his nose against the cold windowpane, trying to see where the man had gone. When he heard footsteps on the front porch, he knew it was too late to call his parents. His knees grew weak as he listened for a knock on the front door, but there was none.

He went to the bed and shook Al one more time to wake him as he whispered, "Al, I tell you there is someone out there."

Al grunted. "What's wrong with you? Git back in bed." He turned over and went back to sleep.

Charlie returned to the window as he heard steps again on the porch. The man was leaving, making his way back to the road, but the strange load was gone. The man disappeared back across the hill in the same direction from which he had come.

Charlie turned slowly and saw the old bed and furnishings in the large, musty bedroom. The moonlight struck the end of the bed and reached across the room almost to the door. The floorboards creaked loudly as he managed to take one step. He closed his eyes and asked if this could be happening. He opened his eyes, and, with one big leap, he jumped into bed beside Al.

The hours passed slowly, and sleep refused to come as Charlie's mind raced over what he had seen. The moments were long, counted only by the steady tap, tap by the limb upon the frost-covered windowpane. When a figure appeared dressed in white standing at the foot of the bed, he sat bolt upright. When his eyes cleared, he realized it was his mother, Nancy, dressed in her nightcap and gown. She held out her arms as if to pull him to her.

"I didn't mean to startle you, Charlie, honey. Don't you think it's time to get up?" she said.

Charlie crawled down to the bottom of the bed and fell into her outstretched arms.

"Did you sleep well?" she asked.

Charlie held tightly to her gown. "Mama, I must have had a wicked dream." He was still holding on to her as they started down the stairs.

Nancy looked back and called, "Al, honey, it's time to get up." She turned back to Charlie. "Why are you acting so strange this morning? Is it the bad dream you had?"

Charlie's grandfather, George, who lived with them, was already up and dressed. He placed another log on the fire in the fireplace and looked up as Charlie entered the room. "Good morning. Merry Christmas Charlie."

"Good morning and Merry Christmas, Paw Paw."

"Hurry and get your chores done. After breakfast we will have some Christmas surprises. I can't wait, can you? One will be a piece of your mom's Christmas fruitcake. Your dad is already out at the barn. Now skedaddle out there and help him."

"I can't wait for the cake," Charlie said as he climbed back up to his bedroom.

"I was beginning to think you boys were gonna sleep till you got bed sores," George said as the smell of the stuffed goose cooking on the spit in the kitchen fireplace permeated the room.

"I'm glad Father killed and picked that old goose," Charlie told his grandpa from the stairs. "He chased me every time I went to the barn or the outhouse."

"I suppose you can think of him every time you put your head on your new pillow. Your mom saved the feathers to make you a soft goose-down pillow."

Charlie turned and hurried up to his room. Mrs. Silver stopped her work in the kitchen and called upstairs, "Hurry and get dressed and do your chores while I make breakfast."

Al was already up. Both boys rushed to get dressed and out to the barn to milk and feed the cows.

As they dashed out the door, Charlie told Al, "I hope old Bossy will give her milk quickly today so we can get back and open our presents."

Nancy shouted after them, "Your dad took the milk bucket with him."

The year was 1824, and it would be a Christmas Charlie would long remember.

Charlie had already made up his mind that he would not tell anyone what he'd seen; after all it could have actually been a dream.

When he and Al had finished their chores and eaten a hurried breakfast, Jacob said, "Let's all go into the front room."

They all went to the front room, where there was a little pine tree decorated with fruit and popcorn. All six children had gathered;

Charlie, Margaret, and Alfred were sitting on a bench, and John, Milton, and Rachel were sitting on the floor.

Nancy wiped her hands on her apron as she left the kitchen and announced, "Rachel gets to give out the presents this year."

Grandpa George motioned with his arm. "Nancy come on and find a place to set."

Then Jacob handed the Bible to Charlie." I am going to ask Charlie to read the Christmas story to us now because we are celebrating Jesus's birthday."

Charlie read from the Bible and then handed it back to his father. Jacob led the family in prayer, thanking God for sending His Son and Savior—the greatest gift of all. When the amen was said, he looked up and told Rachel, "You can give out the presents now."

She scrambled to get the packages. "These are from Mama," she said, giving each of the children a present.

They opened their gifts to find she had knitted everyone a nice pair of wool socks. There was much excitement as they continued to unwrap their other gifts. The girls got shuck dolls, and the little boys got beautiful tops that Grandpa had whittled from cherry wood.

Grandpa slowly stood, made his way over to his bed near the fireplace, and pulled out a large present from under it. "This is for Charlie. I think it's a present we will all get to enjoy." He handed it to Charlie.

"Thank you, Paw Paw," Charlie said as he nervously unwrapped the string and cloth from his gift. He let out a yell. "Oh, it's a fiddle! It's a fiddle! Oh, thank you, Paw Paw. Look, there is even a book on how to learn to play."

Charlie laid the fiddle down and went over and gave his Paw Paw a loving hug. Then he went back and picked up the fiddle. Everyone gathered around to see it as Charlie took the bow and made a few mournful sounds.

Grandfather George interrupted, "It will take a lot of practice to make it sound good, son, but don't neglect your chores while you are learning to play."

"Oh, I won't, I promise!"

Grandfather George continued, "You almost didn't get that fiddle for Christmas. I ordered it down at the general store from a catalogue Mr. Miller had there on the counter. He told me he would bring it to me as soon as it came. Well, it came late yesterday afternoon, and he delivered it during the night. He left it on the front porch. He slipped a note under the door. I found it this morning. He had to wait until he closed the store to bring it. He knew I wanted it for your Christmas present, so he made sure we got it."

"My dream was real!" Charlie said with a happy smile.

"Yes, we know you've always wanted one," Jacob commented.

"Yes, but I mean I watched Mr. Miller come down the hill last night. He scared me half to death. I thought what I saw might just have been a bad dream or a ghost or goblin."

"I bet you never thought he could be delivering your Christmas present, did you?" Nancy said with a smile.

"That is sorta like Saint Nick, bringing gifts at night, ain't it, Mama?" Rachel said as she looked up from playing with her new shuck doll.

They had a wonderful Christmas, and Charlie started learning to play the fiddle, but there were times he was asked to go outside on the porch due to the off-key screeching sounds.

At church he told some of the men he'd been given a fiddle for Christmas, and David Penland and George Grindstaff invited Charlie to come over and practice with them.

"We always have a lot of fun," David said. "Why don't you see if your dad will let you come practice with us?"

Charlie played his fiddle with David and George for several years. His family was glad to see the improvement as he continued to practice in all his spare time. Before long they realized Charlie was really talented and had learned to play very well.

Late one evening Jacob told Charlie and Al, "I have asked John and Tom if they would like to go coon huntin' tonight. Do you boys want to go along?"

The two boys were excited about getting to go hunting.

Jacob, Charlie and Al all headed out with their dogs to go coon hunting with the two men from church, John Wilson and Tom Howell. This was supposed to be a learning experience for the boys and the two dogs, Zeke and Bell. Charlie and Al lit their lanterns and turned down toward Cane Creek.

"Boys, coons like to go to the creek to catch crawdads. Maybe our dogs will pick up a scent there," said Tom, motioning in the direction of the creek.

Soon old Zeke and Bell hit the coon's trail down by the misty creek and bayed at the top of their lungs. The group headed in their direction and started to climb the mountain at the head of Cane Creek. Before long the sound of the dogs seemed to stay in the same place.

"Boys, I think they have treed that rascal!" yelled Tom. He put his hand to his ear and listened intently. "Uh-huh. I can tell from the sound of the dogs. They have a special sound when they tree. You will learn to tell by listening to them. They also bark louder and faster." Tom was in his fifties and was a stout and hardy man. He could outrun or out-walk most hunters, even the young ones. "I think this is fun, don't you Al?" he said, turning to the youngest of the boys.

"Yep. I just hope we get a coon, though," Al replied.

The group pushed their way through the rhododendron bushes and up a steep hill with Tom leading the way. When they reached the top, Tom yelled, "Yep, they've got that old rascal treed! I bet it's the same one that has gotten away from me so many times. Al, hand me that lantern!"

Al passed the lantern to Tom, who held it up, and sure enough they all could see a coon sitting in the forks of the tree. The dogs were barking and jumping up and down trying to climb the tree.

Tom told Jacob, "Take good aim, and shoot that rascal!"

But, just as Jacob lifted his rifle to shoot the coon, it climbed up and into a hole in the tree.

"What do we do now?" John asked.

"There is just one thing. I'll outsmart that coon yet," Tom responded quickly. He took out his knife, cut a forked stick, and started climbing the tree. This excited the dogs even more.

"Are you crazy, Tom? That thing will eat you up!" John yelled.

When he reached the hole, he poked the stick in and started to turn it rapidly. Soon Tom was dragging the coon out of the hole on the end of the stick. When it cleared the hole, Tom held it high in the air and hollered, "Shoot this thing, Jacob, before it eats me up!"

"I can't shoot. I'll hit you!"

"I said shoot it now! He's gonna eat me alive!"

Jacob leaned back, took aim in the darkness, and opened fire on Tom and the coon. Both fell from the tree and landed in the leaves with the dogs. All of a sudden, Tom, the raccoon, and the dogs were in a rip-snorting tussle on the ground at the foot of the tree.

Jacob dropped to his knees and started praying. "Lord, I have killed a man. Oh Lord, what are we going to do? I have killed a man!"

John and Charlie rushed through the bedlam, grabbed Tom by both arms, and dragged him away from the dogs and the coon. Tom moaned and groaned. Al set the lantern down and grabbed both dogs. The coon scampered away as he had done many times before.

The hunters decided to head home with the injured Tom. John and Charlie dragged him along as Al followed with the lantern. Jacob had taken the dogs from Al and rounded up the others' guns.

When Tom finally spoke up, it was to complain. "I don't know how bad I am shot, but you all are killing me dragging me through these saw briars and bushes."

When they finally arrived back at the Silvers' place, Nancy was awakened by the racket and met them at the door.

"Lordy mercy, Jacob, what's happened to Tom?" she asked.

"He's been shot" was Charlie's intense response.

"Who shot him?"

"Dad shot him!" Al answered nervously. "But it was not on purpose, Mom. I'll explain later."

"Get him over here to the bed. Let's see just how serious it is, fellas," Jacob commanded with a shaky voice as he stood the guns in the corner.

"I think it is my leg," said Tom amid his moans and groans.

When the lamplight hit his leg, it revealed one small buckshot in his right leg near his ankle. It was just below the skin. John sterilized his pocketknife over the flame from the lamp and flipped the shot from Tom's leg. He then applied some turpentine, pine rosin, and bandages handed to him by Nancy.

John said wistfully, "I guess this is one hunting trip we will be talking about for a long time. Jacob, I'm not sure this is the way to teach your boys how to hunt."

"Or the dogs either," Jacob added.

Tom said, "As far as I'm concerned, the only bad part about the whole ordeal was that the dratted coon got away. I'd like to catch that rascal. We'll try again soon, boys. I guess we've had enough excitement for one day. We'd better call it a night."

This did not halt Jacob's desire to teach his boys to hunt. He and John took them out pretty often. Tom kept his word too, and they finally caught that coon that had eluded them so many times. They all had mixed feelings when it was finally conquered. Both boys were learning to be good hunters and woodsmen.

The cold winter season soon passed, and spring brought a remarkable beauty to the mountains and the lush green valley below. The kids abandoned their worn shoes as the weather warmed up, freeing their feet at last. The whole family had been working to prepare the ground and doing spring planting.

"You can always tell it's time to plant corn when the oak trees are blooming," said Grandfather George.

It was almost evening on Saturday, and all the children had worked hard during the long day in the field. They had finished their chores of fetching water, feeding the animals, and milking.

Nancy called to them from the back porch, "Boys, I have laid your underclothes, pants, and towels with some soap on your bed."

They took off lickety-split for the bed, picking up their clothes as they headed out the door as fast as their tough, bare feet could carry them. As they reached the dirt road, Charlie looked back over his shoulder with a sheepish grin and yelled, "The last one in is a rotten egg!"

When they turned off the main road onto the worn path that led to their favorite swimming hole, the elderberries and rhododendron blossoms hanging out everywhere seemed to say, "Slow down, you're going to break your necks."

The boys both began throwing their clothes to the wind, and Al hollered to Charlie, "Watch out for that poison oak."

When they reached the massive rock that jutted out into the swift, deep river, they both were stark naked. As they laid the rest of their clothes and towels down, their buttocks glistened like white porcelain just for an instant before both disappeared into the beautiful, clear, cold stream. They came up for air gasping from the cold, and Al let out an excited yell after he finally got his breath.

The two boys frolicked and played in the stream like two young otters, splashing and pushing one another under for a good while. For the boys this place seemed like an enduring part of the land of Eden before the fall of man. This was their favorite place on earth. It belonged to them. It was so refreshing to be there after spending the day toiling in the hot fields, helping their father clear new ground. The swim served both as a fresh, clean bath and as recreation.

Sometimes the neighborhood boys would meet there for a rip-snorting good time on a late summer evening. At other times the whole family would go down to fish. The hole was actually one of their favorite places to fish, and Jacob or Grandpa George would build a roaring fire for them on the riverbank to help attract some catch.

Charlie loved to play in the clear branch of the stream that flowed by their house where the wagons crossed. The cold water felt so good on his bare feet. He also liked to watch the tiny blue butterflies that alit there briefly to get a drink. His other favorite place was the front porch, where he sat with the rest of his family late in the evening, as the cool mist floated down into the valley. They listened to the whip-poorwills and katydids as they volleyed their calls from one side of the mountain to the other.

For Charlie and his family, the seasons came and went with no rush at all. They were mountain people with only time to spend. They were on nature's schedule.

Charlie and his brothers and sisters loved to hear Grandpa tell about how he and his father had served alongside General George Washington for the freedom of the United States. Then Jacob would tell of how he had fought in the Mexican War.

Charlie loved to be outside and smell the rich pine smoke from the kitchen fireplace. It was a signal that supper would soon be ready, and Nancy would be calling them in to eat. Sometimes he even remembered to go to the spring house and get the crock of cold milk without being asked.

Chapter Two

The Saturday evening chores of milking, slopping the pigs, gathering the eggs, and bringing in the wood had all been completed, including bringing in more water from the rock spring house. They'd also placed other wooden buckets of water on the long back porch so the cold water would warm in the bright sun. This water was for the smaller children to get their Saturday night baths.

There was much excitement in the air because Jacob had told them, "If we get our chores done and our baths taken, we will all go to the barnstorming tonight down at Zeb Hutchins's place."

Nancy did not relish the idea of going except to visit with the neighboring ladies.

Charlie was sixteen now and a man by mountain standards. But he and Al headed to the swimming hole for their usual bath in the river. Before long Charlie had crawled out upon the rock with his arms wrapped around his knees and was sitting on his towel, watching his brother as he swam.

"Charlie, I know why you want to go to the barnstorming tonight," Al said.

"Oh yeah? Why do you think I want to go?" he replied sarcastically.

"Throw me the lye soap. It's because the last time we were there, you saw that pretty girl. I know you thought I was going to say so you could show off on your fiddle and banjo, didn't you?"

"Well, maybe so. What's wrong with wanting to see them again? Which one do you think is the purtiest?"

"Mom told me to make sure you wash your hair and behind your ears while you're taking your bath," Al said, then added, "I saw the way they were looking at you the last time we were there."

They continued to talk about girls for a good while until they finished their baths, put on their clothes, and headed back toward the house.

Charlie turned to Al and said, "How did you know why I want to go?"

"I said I saw the way they were looking at you and how you were looking back at them."

"Well, Mr. Alfred, I saw the way you took a gander at those girls from Bandana, and there was more than one of them. I know you say you are too young to be looking at girls, but I don't believe I'm the only one interested in them. There are several who are very pretty, don't you agree? We'd better get a move on because we'll need to help Father gear up the horses and hitch up the wagon so we can get ready to go."

When the two brothers got back home, all the other children had finished their baths and were dressed in their "Sunday go to meeting" clothes. Charlie helped hitch the wagon, and Al helped lay the food basket into it.

Al said, "Mom, these vittles sure do smell good. I can't wait to dig into them!"

Nancy replied, "I do declare, I think all you fellas think about is eating."

"No, Mom, all Charlie thinks about is girls and eating."

The others laughed and made faces at Charlie.

Before long the whole family had loaded into the wagon and was on their way to the community get-together. Nancy had filled her basket with fried chicken, gravy, and biscuits along with her famous apple stack cake, and she had covered the basket with a pretty, hand woven tablecloth. She was looking forward to seeing her neighbors and finding out all the things that had been going on in the area since she had last seen them. This was a festive occasion where they could take time out from their hard work and enjoy lots of good music. Part of the enjoyment came from the fellowship as well as the mouthwatering food each family brought.

Charlie's little sister, Rachel, asked him as the wagon jostled along, "Charlie, will you sing us your silly song?"

He smiled at her and said, "I thought you'd never ask. I'll do it just for you." He took out the fiddle and struck a chord.

> "I've got a big, fat brother, we look like one another.
> And the folks around can't tell us two apart.
> He thinks it's mighty funny to go around borrowing money
> And have the folks chase me around to collect his borrowed debt."

Here he put on a mournful tone for the next couple of lines.

> "The girl I was to marry couldn't tell us two apart.
> She went 'n' married my brother, Jim, and it nearly broke my heart."

He begins to sob.

> "But believe me I got even with my brother Jim.
> I died about a week ago, and they went and buried him!"

The whole wagon was filled with laughter as they rolled along. When they finally pulled into the large barnyard, there was already a sizable crowd of people, and festivity filled the air. Lively music was coming from the gigantic barn, and people were arriving from all directions. The owners had swept the barnyard clean and put hay and planks down in certain places to keep the visitors from getting into the mud or other things that could be found on the ground in a barnyard.

Nancy was sitting with her husband in front of the buckboard. She turned to her children and said quietly, "Now remember who you are, and don't forget to mind your manners."

Jacob said, "Charlie, grab both your instruments, and get in there and help with the music. Sounds to me as though they could use it. I know you're dying to play. Also let me remind both you boys there will be some fellas drinking corn squeezing here tonight, and I don't like y'all coming home with the awful smell of liquor on your breath, is that understood? Do I make myself clear?"

As Charlie grabbed his banjo and fiddle, he quickly replied with some haughtiness, "Yes Pa, I promise."

The settlers who came across the Blue Ridge Mountains brought with them a lot of their own traditions. These included house raising, barn raising, corn shucking, and helping each other at hog-killing time—and almost any other time when extra laborers were needed. The mountain saying was, "That's what neighbors are for."

With these traditions came the fiddle, or "devil's box" as some of the preachers would call it. Also a lot of these gatherings involved drinking moonshine. A part of the tradition that came along with these early settlers was the making of these spirits. At various corn shucking's, a jug of liquor was hidden in the middle of the pile of corn, and the first person to get to it as they shucked was the winner; however, they had to share it with others.

The circuit-riding preachers who served the little churches, like Reverend Thomas, spoke vehemently against the ungodly barn dances, worldly music, and frolicking as well as the drinking that took place here in these mountains. But the making of moonshine was a source of income for many of the mountain men. Sipping at the devil's brew was nothing new to Charlie and Al. They had sampled it long before without their dad knowing.

Nancy was an extremely devout Christian and would often quote the scripture: "Woe to the man who puts the bottle to his brother's mouth." She would also say, "God did not make a praying knee and a dancing foot on the same person."

They all knew drinking the devil's mixture was definitely not approved of in their home.

Charlie Silver was a strong, handsome sixteen-year-old and was a perfect example of the rugged mountain breed. He was not afraid of hard work. This was something he had learned from his father and his grandfather. He was tall and had black curly hair and a dark complexion.

Charlie had rough mountain manners. He also had three other qualities that made him well-liked by the entire community. First he had a pleasant disposition, which included a radiant and warm smile. He was known to be easygoing and, therefore, was admired by his elders as well as many of the youth in his community. Second Charlie was also well known when it came to making merriment, for he was usually the life of the party. It was said he could play the fife better than anyone in these parts. Third he was well respected by the other men as a budding expert when it came to chopping wood and help-ing make barns, houses, and fences. He was even good at laying stone with mud to build fireplaces and stone fences. As an avid hunter, Charlie helped provide much meat for the family table.

Zeb Hutchins and his son were already lighting oil lanterns and hanging them on the rail fence posts so guests could see how to get up the slope and into the barn loft. A greeting line was forming as the people slowly made their way up the hill. Charlie was making a run up when a group of three girls joined him. As the old saying goes, many of them had set their hats for him. They thought he was the most handsome man in the valley. He greeted them smiling and answered their questions as they followed him into the open barn loft. It was hard to tell who was more excited—Charlie or the girls.

The barn loft had split-log benches around the outside walls and a platform at the far end. As they walked in, they also noticed several large tables had already been filled with delicious mountain cooking. Charlie carried his fiddle and banjo, and when David Penland who was busy tuning his instrument looked up and saw him, he yelled, "We can make music now—Charlie is here!"

There was a general consensus that Charlie was already an accomplished musician. He knew how to make sure everyone had a good time and was usually the center of attention, especially with the youth of the community.

Charlie bounded onto the hay-filled stage, laid his banjo on the straw, and took out his fiddle from its old, worn case. He was an expert with it and had already won several fiddling competitions. Charlie liked to announce that he was not the only one who enjoyed the instrument—Thomas Jefferson and Davy Crockett were both excellent fiddle players.

The music group included Thomas Howell on the dulcimer, David Penland on the mandolin, George Grindstaff on the guitar, Isaac Baker on the banjo, and, of course, Charlie on the fiddle. Charlie gave a nod to the rest of the group, indicating he had finished tuning his fiddle.

George Grindstaff called out, "Let's start with *The Old Cackling Hen.*" The music began to sound throughout the dimly lit loft. Many in the audience sat on the sturdy benches while others stood quietly talking to each other. As the music ended, they gave the musicians rousing applause.

Someone then yelled, "Play *Cripple Creek*!" When it was completed, the audience again showed their appreciation, and the musicians began playing *Soldiers' Joy*. As this tune got underway, several couples went out to the front and began dancing. The atmosphere became even livelier when the small band began to play the number *Turkey in the Straw*.

While Charlie was playing, he happened to glance up and see Barbara and Isaiah Stuart along with their daughter, Francis, making their way into the loft and greeting many people. He could not keep his eyes off Francis or keep his thoughts on his music. She was wearing a pretty gingham dress, and she seemed to float as she entered the room. It seemed strange to Charlie that he had not noticed her before. She had grown up without him noticing it; she certainly did not look like the same little girl.

Charlie had known Francis for a long time—ever since she and her family had moved to the opposite side of the mountain. It was not far from where he lived. They'd moved there from down east in Anson County when she was only six years old. Charlie and Francis attended the quaint little one-room school together. He was only able to attend occasionally, though, because he had to help his pa on the farm. He did not get to go regularly like Francis.

Times were changing for them. Many of these mountain people had started realizing their children needed to be able to read and write, especially so they could read the Bible. Charlie could read the Bible now and write some, but Francis had learned to read and write very well. Jacob had once told his family, "I want all my family to be book read because they may be called to preach someday. I wish I had been able to go to school and learnt to read and write. Thank the good Lord for Nancy, who helps me a lot."

The host of the party hollered, "I guess everyone is here, and the table has some mighty fine-looking fixings. Sakes alive, I believe it's time to eat. I believe some of you druther eat than listen to these fellas make music. Brother Green, will you ask the blessing for us?"

After the lengthy blessing by Brother Green, someone shouted, "Dig in." People gathered around the table and began filling their tin plates with a variety of delicious food, then found places to sit and talk with their neighbors as they ate.

Charlie was surrounded by several men near the stage. They told him how much they enjoyed his fiddle playing. Then their conversation shifted to hunting and fishing. They had a hard time talking with him because he was distracted and continued to gaze in the direction of Francis and her mother. He was relieved when the conversation ended. Francis had already filled her plate and had found a place to sit, so he hurried to grab some food and dashed over to sit with her.

As he approached her, he said, "I don't suppose you remember me. I'm Charlie Silver. I haven't seen you in a coon's age. Do you mind if I have a seat beside you?"

"I know who you are, Charles Silver. And yes, I would be pleased to have you eat with me," she replied with a sweet smile.

Charlie started to eat then stopped. "This food is delicious. Are you having fun?"

"Yes I am, it is a nice party with good food and good music. It is good to see you again Charlie."

"Do you remember Mrs. Mae Porter, our schoolteacher?" Charlie asked.

"Yes, she was a good teacher. I liked her a lot."

"Do you remember when the boys went hog wild and were fighting? It was over a pocketknife. Harold Hudgins had his out and poked Homer Lawson in the bunkum, and it was on." They both laughed.

"Mrs. Porter huffed and puffed and put her hands on her hips and said, 'We will not have any more of this kind of carrying on in here. We are here to learn! Do you want me to tell your fathers what has happened here today?' Both Homer and Harold begged her not to mention it to their dads." Frankie recalled.

Charlie said, "She gave them both a good whooping."

"That stopped them from cutting any more shines in her class-room." Frankie said..

The two talked about going to school together and the scrumptious food as they were eating.

"Would you like to have a piece of the pumpkin cake I made?" Francis asked.

"Yes, I'd be much obliged, thank you."

She took Charlie's plate, cut him a piece of her cake, and brought it back to him. Charlie got up, filled two cups with apple cider from the large, wooden barrel, and brought one to Francis.

"I love this cake. It is delicious," he told her. "You are a great cook."

"I sweetened it with 'lasses and honey."

"It sure is good," Charlie commented as he ate. "I hope they didn't spike this cider, don't you?" He added softly. "I promised my dad I wouldn't drink tonight."

They both laughed.

Francis told him, "I can't help but notice how the other girls are looking at you and trying to get your attention. You seem to be very popular. You have them wrapped around your little finger."

"Yeah, I suppose, but they are not as pretty as you. Pay them no mind."

They were just getting comfortable talking with each other when Aunt Polly yelled, "Fellas, all right, why don't we have some more of that good old mountain music? It'll help our food digest better!"

Charlie pretended not to hear and continued talking with Francis.

One of his fellow musicians called out, "Charlie, come on—that is if you can stop courting long enough!"

Everyone laughed, and this seemed to embarrass Frances. Her face turned red, and she looked down at the floor.

Charlie told her, "Don't let them bother you. They just like to aggravate me. Could I see you again after we finish playing?"

Francis smiled and nodded her head.

After several more songs, the ladies began packing the leftovers in their baskets and placed them on the table so the men could carry them to their wagons and buggies.

Then Zeb Hutchins yelled, "Okay, folks, let's have some dancing. Grab your partner and let's have a little do-si-do square dancing. I will call it. How about playing *Boil Them Cabbage Down*?"

So many people came to dance, the whole barn shook. When they finished, Zeb called out, "We will have a cake and pie auction. The ladies have made some good cakes and pies. Some of them have been cut, but there are plenty left, and they don't want to take them home. The money we raise will go to our school."

Charlie bid on Francis's pumpkin cake and ended up buying it for three bits. Some of the men bid on their own wives' pies and cakes.

The musicians started playing again and finished the evening with another lively hoedown. Finally they put their instruments away in their worn cases. People milled around and gave their well wishes before departing for home.

Charlie passed his mom and told her to get his cake and put it in her basket. He made a bee line for Frances and asked if he could take her basket to her wagon.

As he lifted the basket, Barbara said, "Well, Charlie, how nice of you to take our basket." Francis followed him as he took it outside.

"Where is your dad's wagon, Francis?" he asked.

"It's over there by that tree."

He rushed over, placed the basket in the wagon, and turned back toward Francis as she approached him.

"I am wondering if I might walk you home tonight," he said.

"Well, I don't mind, but you'll have to ask my pa if it's all right with him."

Charlie was so relieved because he had been afraid she would say no. He knew most girls said no because they didn't want to play easy to get.

When they asked Isaiah, Francis's father, he said sternly, "Why don't the two of you ride home with us in our wagon? That's a long walk."

Charlie said, "That's all right."

"We don't mind." Came Frankie's response.

Isaiah reluctantly gave his consent. "You'll need to carry our lantern. Here, I'll light it for you." He handed it to Charlie.

When they had started on their walk home, Francis looked up at Charlie and said, "I enjoyed the music tonight. You have a special talent."

Before long they were overtaken by Isaiah and Barbara on their way home.

Francis called out, "See you at the house."

Barbara replied, "You two be careful, honey."

Charlie said, "You were saying you enjoyed the music and my playing. Thank you so much for that compliment, Francis. Do you mind if I call you Frankie instead of Francis? I noticed that is what your brother, Blackston, called you."

"Well that's what I'm used to, except when they are mad at me."

"Ma and Pa call Alfred 'Al' until they get upset with him about something. When they're upset, you can hear them call, 'Alfred, git yourself in here!'"

They both laughed as they walked on toward Frankie's house.

"Frankie, I don't see why we need this lantern. Don't you think the moon is bright enough tonight?" Charlie asked.

"Yes. You can blow it out if you've a mind to."

"I love to smell the fresh woods. Don't you think they seem to smell better at night?"

Frankie responded, "My favorite is the smell of a cornfield at night in the fall."

Charlie added, "Or the smell of molasses being made in the fall."

They continued on their way, laughing and talking. Their time together went so fast. Before they got in sight of the house, Charlie stopped and lit the lantern again. Taking Frankie by the hand, he whispered, "I would like to see you again soon—that is if you don't mind."

They were nearing Frankie's house, so they slowed their pace.

"Well, there is going to be a revival at the church next week. Ma and Pa plan to go." Frankie looked into his eyes and said, "Why don't you come? It starts tomorrow night."

"That sounds good to me. I'll see you there then. What time does it start?"

"At seven o'clock."

As they reached the top of the steps, Charlie handed Frankie the lantern, and the light revealed Isaiah standing in the doorway.

Charlie said, "Good night, Frankie. See you later. Good evening, Mr. Stuart. Thanks for letting Frankie walk home with me." Charlie quickly dashed down the rock steps.

The skipping of Charlie Silver on the dirt road with his big brogan shoes interrupted the quietness of this pleasant spring night. He was happy and had good reason to be. The full moon shone almost as brightly as full daylight, and to him the whole world seemed to be growing brighter with each step he took. He was in love! Yes, she had to be the one for him. There was no doubt.

Charlie was a remarkably handsome young man with broad, muscular shoulders and a pleasing personality. He, like his dad, was about six feet tall and strong with black hair, dark blue eyes, and a dark complexion. He'd grown up helping his father in this little corner of Burke County and had grown from a stout mountain boy into a tough young man. Some people called Charlie a dreamer, but others saw him as a talented and ambitious young adult. Charlie continued his long walk home. He tucked his thumbs under the galluses of his clean, homespun britches. He began to whistle a tune as he walked back toward home. It was not terribly far.

Suddenly clouds hid the moon, making it pitch dark, as if someone had decided to turn out the lights. He stumbled along, hoping he was still on the narrow road. He decided to whistle again as he walked. He thought this would keep him from feeling anxious and would also break the silence. He was not afraid, but the sound of his whistling eased his tense mood.

In an instant something hit him hard on the chest, and he fell backward onto the road. His first thought was that a mountain lion or a bear had attacked him, or maybe someone was spoiling for a good fight—after all he had just walked the most beautiful girl in the neighborhood home. In any case he was scared. Then he felt something licking him on the face and realized it was his hunting dog, old Zeke. The dog had probably heard him whistling and had come to greet him.

"Zeke, where in the world did you come from? You scared me half to death!" Charlie sighed in sheer relief. This was certainly a welcome and pleasant surprise. As the clouds moved away, the silver moon came out, lighting the spring night. He lay there looking up at the moon with his dog breathing heavily in his face.

Charlie and Zeke got up and continued toward home. It did not surprise Charlie to find the lights out. Everyone had gone to bed— even Mama, who was always last to turn in after patching clothes or churning. Charlie did not realize it was past midnight. He decided to go to the back side of the house and crawl through a tiny dining room window without waking his mom and dad. As he raised the window and started to creep through, he felt something on his forehead.

A low voice said quietly, "Move another inch, and you are dead as a doornail!"

"Mom, it's me, Charlie. Don't shoot!" he yelled nervously.

"Oh my Lord, son, you should know better!" Her voice broke as she lowered the pistol.

"But Mom, I didn't want to wake up the whole house."

"That might be better than getting yourself killed, young man!"

Jacob was now lighting the oil lamp on the large dining room table as Charlie finished sliding through the small window.

"What in tarnation is causing all the commotion out here? Can't a person get some sleep?" Jacob grunted as Nancy placed the small pistol on the table near the lamp.

Trying to relieve the tension, she asked Charlie, "Are you hungry, son? There are some cold biscuits and honey and a dab of butter under that tablecloth, but don't leave a gom on the table when you're finished."

Charlie took a tin plate from the corner cupboard, stirred the honey and butter together, and made himself a tasty snack. He poured some water and ate the honey and biscuits. He couldn't help but think of what a night he'd had. It was as though the world was spinning too fast. He was excited and nervous now—yes, extremely jittery. Something different had awakened inside him.

After Charlie had finished the victuals and gulped down a dipper of water, he told his mom and dad good night and turned in for the night. As he lay in bed, he found he could not get the beautiful Frankie off his mind. She was stunning; yes, she was very special. Over and over in his mind, he saw her as she moved in and out of the crowd. She was an angel sent from heaven.

Charlie rolled and tumbled on his straw tick and fought sleep as he went over all the happenings of the day. Most nights his thoughts would be on his music or work for the next day, but not tonight. Al was already sound asleep and gulped for air occasionally.

Charlie invited his best friend, Joshua Biddix, to go to the revival meeting with him. As they walked together to the little log church at Loafers Glory, Charlie could not help but feel this might be his lucky night, although he certainly would not admit it to anyone—except maybe to Josh. His real purpose in going was not to hear the preaching of God's word but to see the most beautiful girl in the world.

He and Josh sauntered into the church and took a seat on one of the rough, slatted benches. The church was dimly lit inside with just a few candles and oil lamps. Everyone turned slowly, trying not to be obvious, to check out the two visitors.

The preacher welcomed them with a friendly gesture and a smile. He said, "We would like to welcome our visitors."

The choir began to sing, and the pastor seemed to notice the inattentiveness of his two visitors in his little congregation. This distraction continued as he began to preach his sermon. He preached louder but the louder he preached, the further Charlie's mind was from the sermon and God's word. He had spotted Frankie sitting with the choir. To him this was much more appealing than hellfire and damnation. The two exchanged glances, and finally Charlie mustered up enough courage to smile at her. Meanwhile Josh had his eye on a girl who was also singing in the choir. With a couple of consenting nods, the two boys agreed to look into this matter as soon as the service ended. It seemed to take forever.

Charlie and Josh waited for the two girls to come out of the church afterward. In the complete darkness, Charlie made a big blunder. He was extremely nervous anyway, but it was not long before he realized he had asked the wrong girl if he could see her home, and Josh had ended up walking Frankie home. Josh was, of course, delighted with the outcome.

When the two boys met on the road later, after walking the girls home, they discussed what had happened. When Josh commented on the beautiful blonde he had taken home, Charlie nearly exploded into a rage. He told Josh he had realized it right after they had left, but he could not tell the other girl he did not mean to ask to walk her home.

The next night Charlie was much more cautious when they returned to the revival meeting. He and Josh already had a clear understanding that Charlie would be the one who would take

Frankie home afterward. It took a lot of explaining before she would consent after the episode the night before. She asked Josh if what Charlie had said was true, and Josh explained it had all been a big mistake.

During the rest of their courtship, Charlie and Frankie had many good laughs about his taking the wrong girl home. Frankie never told Charlie how upset and green with envy she had become. She had been convinced he would ask her. When she realized what had happened, she had been extremely relieved it had actually been a mistake. After that second night, Charlie spent many happy hours in that little church and community with Frankie and her parents.

Fall arrived, and Charlie invited Frankie and her family to come over and watch him and his family make molasses. He told her, "it's an annual occasion, and many in the area help with the chore. 'Lasses and honey are the only things Mom uses to sweeten our food. You'll need to come, 'cause it's a big affair. Many of the folk around grow cane and bring it on their sleds to our 'lasses mill at the close of the day. There we grind out the juice and boil it until it becomes golden 'lasses. Have you ever seen it being made?"

"No, Charlie, I haven't, but it sounds like fun."

"Well, Frankie, that is when the festive gathering takes place. The men have specific jobs. John will stir the 'lasses to keep it from burning and sticking to the pan. Another man, Oscar, keeps the fire under the enormous pan poked and stirred. And I, with the help of a mule, feed the cane into the huge rollers to squeeze out the juice. The mule is tied to a long pole attached to the huge grinder—the pole leads him around and around. You'd better wear a coat 'cause this work often goes on until after midnight. My Lordy mercy, I have talked too much. I'll just show you all about it when you come."

When Frankie and her parents arrived at the 'lasses mill, she went over to talk to Charlie where he was grinding the juice from the cane. She did not see the mule coming around in a circle. Charlie had to drop the handful of cane he was feeding into the mill and grab Frankie to keep the mule and the pole from hitting her.

He said, "Well, that was some way to get a hug. You could have been hurt if that pole had hit you in the head."

They both looked into each other's eyes and laughed.

Frankie said, "You were faster than greased lightning. You scared me half to death. I guess that's better than being knocked backward and landing on my bunkum in front of everyone."

"I believe it will be safer if you go sit down by the boiler where the others are sitting. I will be through here in a jiffy, and I'll come down to be with you."

The warm steam and the sweet smell of the molasses in the cool fall night gave a special mood to this gathering. The loud laughter of Aunt Polly could be heard up the valley over the other visitors'. Several people sopped up some of the golden sticky stuff with short pieces of cane.

Someone commented, "This gives me a hankering for a dab of butter and a hot biscuit."

They all laughed.

"Well, you don't say. Next time I'll have to bring ya some," Aunt Polly said in a thunderous voice.

Charlie finished grinding the cane and went to join Frankie and her parents.

"Thank you for saving me," Frankie said when he sat down.

"It happens a lot. People don't see the mule coming. I'm glad you came."

"It looks like it is hard work, but everyone helps out," Frankie said enthusiastically.

Several times Jacob told Charlie to go get another bucket of juice from the mill and pour it into the wooden barrel, which had a hand-made spigot that fed the juice into a large pan. Charlie obeyed but gave his father an unhappy and begrudging look.

"Evening, Mr. and Mrs. Stuart. Thanks for bringing Frankie to see us make 'lasses."

Isaiah said, "Nothing would keep her from coming. I think there is something sweet here besides the 'lasses."

Aunt Polly said loudly, "There's nothing like young love, but it sure can get you in a heap of trouble. Ain't that right, ladies?"

The other ladies looked at her not knowing how they should answer.

Charlie smiled as he told Isaiah, "Remind me to give you a jar of 'lasses before you leave. I'm going to do everything to sweeten you and Mrs. Stuart up as well as I can."

This time Charlie gladly rode home with the Stuarts in their wagon. He and Frankie crawled into the back after his hard day of making molasses. He was not thinking about his tiredness. Just being with her rejuvenated his whole body. He did not even dread the long walk back home.

Chapter Three

On a beautiful spring day in May 1830, the relentless blast of a distant hunting horn echoed through the Toe River Valley. As the sound came closer, Charlie Silver realized it was the Baptist Circuit Riding Preacher coming through the community. The horn was his way of reminding folks of Charlie's wedding to Frankie Stuart that same afternoon.

Charlie was putting the finishing touches on a small log house that would be his and Frankie's. He wanted everything to be just right when he carried her over the threshold of their new home.

Charlie worked hard, and he began to sing a happy tune. He had every reason in the world to be happy he had won the hand of the most beautiful girl in the area, and she would become his wife that very day. As his mind drifted away from his work to Frankie, the sweet smell of horse apple blossoms floated down from the gentle hillside, making him feel dizzy. He stepped over to the spring to get a refreshing drink of cold water, using the gourd dipper hanging there.

Everything seemed to be perfect; it was the most beautiful spring day he had ever seen in his entire life. He had worked hard on the house during the day and sometimes on into the night, so he was now dead tired. Finally he decided to succumb to the blissfulness of the day, and he lay down on the velvety green moss under the gigantic oak that stood by the bold spring. Doing so, he fell asleep with his old straw hat shielding his face from the bright light.

While he was resting, he began thinking of the first time he had taken notice of Frankie at the barnstorming. It was there she had made her first lasting impression.

Charlie had spent many happy hours and days with Frankie. She, in turn, had had many happy Sunday visits with the Silver family. They had all grown extremely fond of her. She had the full support of Charlie's brother, Al, and his father, and that had helped tremendously with their loving relationship. The more time Charlie spent with Frankie, the more he wanted to be around her. There was no doubt about it: they were in love!

Finally, one night on her front porch, he worked up enough courage to ask Frankie to marry him. She consented but told Charlie he would need to ask her father and mother for their permission. Nervous and shaky, he asked Isaiah and Barbara for their daughter's hand in marriage. Isaiah refused at first, but with Barbara's help Charlie convinced him he should not stand in their way. Isaiah realized she might just take off with Charlie sometime without his consent or his even knowing about it, like one of her friends had done recently. With much hesitation he gave them his permission and blessing.

They had set the date for sometime in May to give Charlie enough time to build a log house in the little cove given to him by his father.

The neighbors came from far and near for the house raising. They had a big log rolling. They helped fell, hue, notch, and pin the logs. His father was handy with the mallet and froe and made hand-split oak shingles for the roof of the house and both porches. Grandpa George walked over to lend a hand and kept telling Charlie how proud he was to see him taking on the responsibilities of a grown man. Building a new house took a long time, but not half as long when there was plenty of help.

The women of Charlie's church showed up with baskets of food for the workers. They later assisted his mother in arranging the hand-made things they had made for them. They had all gotten together and had a quilting bee, making several beautiful quilts that would come in handy on the cold winter nights in the mountains.

Frankie had not actually seen the house; it was to be a surprise for her. Charlie had promised he would make the little house just as she wanted. Everyone was happy for them, but not nearly as happy as Charlie and Frankie.

Suddenly Charlie awoke to the loud, deep voice of Preacher Thomas. He was a short, stocky, round man with deep-set eyes, drooping shoulders, and bright-red cheeks. He was a jovial man and always wore a large, broad-rimmed black hat.

Jacob always told his family, "Preacher Thomas serves these mountain people only as a true man of God could do."

He was well liked and revered by the entire Silver family.

"Well, is this how you plan to spend your married life?" Preacher Thomas said, waking Charlie. "You'd better get on your feet!"

Charlie lurched to the side, throwing the hat off his face to discover the old preacher sitting on his horse and looking down with a big smile.

"Well...well...you see, I guess I fell—" Charlie grunted as he got to his feet.

"Oh, I know," said Preacher Thomas. "You're resting for the big occasion. Well, you'd better rest, 'cause you will need it. This will probably be the last time in your life you'll get to lie around like this. How's the house coming?"

"It's about finished thanks to all the help from our neighbors and friends. I guess you could say your sermons on loving your neighbor as yourself have boosted the spirit of helpfulness. We have had a passel of people working for about a week. Even Grandpa has helped some."

"I hope they have been listening to my sermons. Sometimes I wonder. I often say they have selective hearing. At least they heed what they want to heed."

"Everyone has been right neighborly. As soon as I finish hanging the back door, it will be ready. I just got the hinges from Israel Boone, the blacksmith who lives over in Burnsville. He made them for me. He also made a crane and two pot hooks for our new fireplace. He gave me a set of dog irons for the fireplace as a weddin' present. Putting the hinges on won't take long. Do you think Frankie will like it, Preacher?"

"I see no reason why not, since most girls have to live with their mother-in-law and father-in-law for a spell before they have the luxury of living in their own home," said Preacher Thomas.

"Well, I'd better get to work on that door. It won't finish itself, and besides, it will soon be time for me to get ready to go to Frankie's house. I hope Father will have the buggy hitched up before I get there. He and the rest of the family are going in the buckboard. I hope there won't be a crowd. I'll see you at three o'clock sharp."

"Now, don't you go by George Young's place before you come. I don't want to marry you two with the smell of liquor on your breath."

"Oh, don't worry about that, Preacher. My brother may have to hold me up, but it won't be because I'm drunk. I'll be there and soberer than ever."

"I still have a few shut-ins to visit today before the wedding. Don't forget what I told you." Preacher Thomas laughed as he rode off down the trail.

The cabin had one big room. Charlie planned to add another section later on with a dog run in between the two. One room would be used for a kitchen and the other for a bedroom. There were no real windows, just a flat, wide board that slid open for fresh air. This board had a hole for a peg to keep it closed. There were two small porches, one on the front looking down the valley and a very small one outside the door at the back. It had large, flat rocks for steps in the front and back. The smell of fresh-cut timber permeated the room.

Charlie finished the door and then walked up through the apple orchard to the top of the ridge, toward his father's house. He reached the top of the hill and stopped. He stood there looking down at his family's large log house. He had spent many happy and precious days there as a little lad. Then he turned his eyes to the small church standing nearby and remembered his appointment for the afternoon. He looked back at the little house he had just left.

He was extremely eager to start his married life with his new bride. His childhood had been terrific, but a whole new world seemed to be awakening for him. A dream he had dreamed for several years was about to come true.

As he was standing there looking down, a voice interrupted his thoughts. It was his stepmother, a stout woman in her late fifties. To Charlie she was next to the most delightful and sweet woman in the world. Charlie had not been fortunate enough to know his real mother, but Nancy had been a caring and loving mother to him. She was proud of Charlie and was glad he was taking such a momentous step. She was getting gray, and her face showed lines from the hard work and distress that had been so prevalent during most of her married life.

Nancy was standing on the front porch calling, "Charlie! Dinner!"

He acknowledged her by waving his hat high in the air as he began to descend the steep slope through the sweet-smelling apple trees. Upon reaching the first step of the house, he could feel the excitement in the air. This was a historic occasion for the entire family. Charlie would be the first child to get married.

As he entered the house, he saw his brother, William, in the old wooden bathtub. William was the youngest member of the family. He was nearly a year old and was always the last in the tub. His big sister, Margaret, age fifteen, was scrubbing him as he squirmed about in the soapy water. Al, now fourteen, John, age twelve, Milton, age ten, Rachel, age nine, Lucinda, age four, and Marvel Alexander, age three, all had been scrubbed from head to foot and had donned their best homespun clothes.

After taking William from the bathwater and drying him, Margaret helped him dress. When he was ready, Jacob called the family to the table.

Jacob was a deeply religious man and an active member of the Baptist church near the house. He had been called to preach and sometimes filled in when Preacher Thomas couldn't make it. He also filled in at other nearby churches and refused to take anything as payment. He could not read the Bible, so Nancy would read the verses for him, and he would memorize them for his sermon. Jacob was always ready with a message just in case he was needed.

When everyone was seated on the benches around the big table, Jacob asked them to bow their heads as he prayed.

"Dear Lord and our heavenly Father, thank you for our family, and help us to do right by them. Lord, we know this is Charlie's special day. We pray your blessings on his marriage to Frankie, and thank you Lord for her. Thank you for this food provided by your precious hand. Bless it as we are about to partake of it. We know that all blessings do come from you. Amen."

Nancy and Margaret had made a special blackberry cobbler and cooked Charlie's favorite dish: chicken and dumplings. He smiled and looked at his stepmom as he reached for the steaming, scrumptious-smelling dumplings.

"Mom, I hope Frankie can cook like you. You are the best cook in the whole wide world. I hope she knows how to make dumplings like you do."

"Now, Charlie, I'm sure she will be a good cook. After all I didn't learn how to make dumplings until long after your pa and I married. It is true I had a hard time learning to cook like Jacob's mother, and he will vouch for that."

Jacob looked up and commented, "I have to say, she has improved over the years. You know something else? I have learned to be careful when talking about your mom's cookin'."

The whole family laughed except Mrs. Silver, who said, "Okay, y'all, we had better be loadin' up and gettin' on our way if you'ns plan to be at our Charlie's weddin'. Let me remind you, I will not put up with any of you being rambunctious today, is that understood?"

The children rushed to finish eating and then dashed out and climbed into the wagon. Their father had piled straw in the back to make the trip more comfortable. This was a real treat because it was not very often that they got to leave home. It was unusual for them to cross over the big Toe River unless it was for something truly special. They always enjoyed fording the river and watching the water swirl under the wagon as the horses slowly crossed the swift, clear water. There were places where it almost reached into the wagon.

They all remembered sitting by the fireside listening to their father's account of the Cherokee Indian chief's daughter, Estatoe. She had planned to run away with a young brave from the Catawba tribe to the east, but his canoe sank under a fallen log in the river, and he drowned. Upon hearing the story of his death, she drowned herself in the river while mourning her soul mate. Their father always finished the tale by saying, "That was how the Toe River got its name."

Each time they crossed the river, the children imagined the young brave waiting at the water's edge for Estatoe. So the children were wide-eyed with excitement now as their parents got into the wagon. Nancy called back to Charlie, "We'll see you there."

To the children this was much like the trip they had made with their uncle, Benny. He had taken them down to the old general store and bought them horehound candy—a happy and memorable trip they'd talked about for a long time afterward.

Now they rode off and left Charlie standing in the doorway with his shirt off, waving at them. Al hollered from the buckboard, "Don't forget to put some bear grease on your hair! You need to look sharp for the weddin'."

Charlie went back into the house to put on his best shirt and pants.

The Silvers' was not the only house filled with excitement. Frankie was getting ready and was wondering if Charlie would be on time. She hoped everything would go as she had planned. Frankie was a lovely, petite girl with fair skin and flowing blonde hair. She was exceptionally smart. She was a good hand at quilting, spinning, and sewing. Frankie could card and spin as many yards a day as any of the older women. She was not only small and bright, but she possessed all the charms of the fairer sex. Today she would be even lovelier than usual.

Her education was more than the average girl's in these parts. The other women admired her for this. All that was expected of them was to perform chores around the house and to have children. These mountain people considered education to be a luxury, not a necessity. Frankie had walked through rain, snow, and sleet and had worked late at night by the firelight learning to read and write. She had developed a special love for writing poetry.

Her brother, Blackston, had just taken her belongings, including her hope chest, outside and placed them on the front porch. From there they would be loaded into Charlie's buggy when he arrived. Frankie's aunt, Bertha, and her mother were busy working in the house and fixing flower arrangements for this special event.

Frankie walked over to her father, who was sitting on the porch in his gaudy handmade rocking chair, and said, "I did my best, Father. I appreciate your giving in and letting me marry Charlie. You all will have to come visit when you can. I hope you and Mother will be all right after I leave. You have Blackston to help look after you. Now, I don't want you to worry about me."

Isaiah looked up at Frankie and replied, "I believe Charlie will make you a good husband. I know you two love each other very much. I believe you have a fine young man there. Just be a good wife to him in return. I only wish you had waited a few more years, but I suppose love can't wait. That's what your mother and I told our parents. Now, you run along and get into your new dress. I can't wait to take a gander at it. Help Aunt Bertha and your mama get ready for the weddin'. They both are in such a tizzy. I'll keep Charlie's folks and the preacher company out here on the porch when they come."

Frankie stooped and planted a kiss on her father's forehead as a large tear formed in the corner of her eye. Then she hurried into the house. She and her father were extremely close; after all she was his only daughter.

Scarcely had ten minutes lapsed when Isaiah saw a wagonload of happy children laughing and waving. They slowly made their way down the long, dusty road from the top of the mountain.

Mrs. Silver was wearing her new split bonnet and her best "Sunday go to meeting" dress. She glanced back at the children and told them, "Quit cuttin' up and pestering one another. Don't git me riled, or I might just give you a whooping with the leather strop when we git home!"

They remained seated quietly as they pulled up in the Stuarts' yard. As the wagon came to a jostling halt, Frankie's father got up from his rocking chair and walked down the steps and over to the wagon. He extended his hand to Jacob.

"Howdy, Jacob. How are you doing? Are you ready for this to happen?"

Jacob replied, "I'm fair to middling, I suppose. I hope they know what they're doing. I doubt they know what comes along with being old married folks."

They both laughed as Jacob helped his wife down from the wagon. Isaiah started to help the children down. Mrs. Silver came over, extended her hand, and said, "It's good to see you again. It looks like a beautiful day for the weddin'."

"It sure is, ma'am. I'll help the children down for you."

He helped to set the last child down, and then he motioned to them and said, "You folks come on. We can set on the porch a spell before the wedding if you'd like. It may take those women a long time to git ready."

Frankie's mother, Barbara, had heard them arriving and came out on the porch to greet them. She hugged each child and then greeted

Jacob and Nancy. She also welcomed several other neighbors who had come to the wedding along with a couple of Charlie's special friends, including Josh Biddix, who was to be the best man.

Barbara said, "You folks come on in. Frankie's about ready."

She had barely finished saying that when the hollow thumping sound of hoof beats could be heard. A cloud of dust boiled up at the top of the mountain.

"What in tarnation? That looks like a buggy in front with some-one chasing it on horseback," Isaiah said with a questioning look on his face.

Isaiah and Jacob both quickly got out of their chairs and went to the edge of the porch to get a closer look at what was going on. Soon Charlie's buggy came flying into the yard as he yelled, "Whoa, Dan, whoa."

Preacher Thomas came in only a few lengths behind. Both men tied their horses to the rail.

Preacher Thomas looking at Charlie said, "I should have known you would beat me. Besides, your horse knew the way, and mine didn't. You sure made me eat your dust."

They both laughed as they shook hands. Jacob and Isaiah walked down the steps to meet the preacher.

Preacher Thomas said, "Well, it looks as though Charlie has a free weddin' coming to him. We met over there at the crossroads, and Charlie said, 'I'll bet old Dan can beat your horse by a long shot.' Then I said without thinking, 'If you win, your wedding will be free.' I believe I got the worst end of the deal including the dust. At least I gave him a run for his money! I may need to get shed of this old nag, but she has been a good'n. We have covered lots of miles together."

Charlie motioning to the preacher said, "Isaiah, this is Reverend Thomas. Reverend Thomas, Isaiah Stuart."

"Pleased to meet you preacher Thomas."

The preacher continued brushing the dust from his black coat as he asked, "Are y'all ready to get on with this weddin'?"

"We are ready as we'll ever be. In fact I've been ready a long time, Preacher!" came Charlie's quick response.

The four men climbed the steps and entered the house. They found the children seated on the floor and Barbara and Mrs. Silver standing and talking. Then Aunt Bertha, who had been helping Frankie, came out of the bedroom and went straight to the little old pump organ that had been in the family for years. The preacher and Charlie stood near a little table in front of the chairs. Aunt Bertha began pumping and beating out the melody of "Here Comes the Bride" on the dilapidated little organ.

Frankie appeared in the doorway of her bedroom. Charlie's eyes widened, and his mouth dropped open. He was astounded! She was so beautiful and radiant. He was quite convinced that she was the most beautiful girl in the whole world. He tried to manage a smile, but this was too difficult since his mouth was still open.

She was wearing a pretty white dress and holding a small bouquet of pink roses and Queen Anne's lace mixed with dog hobble. Charlie stood in front of the preacher with Josh as Frankie came out and took her father's arm.

They approached Preacher Thomas, who asked, "Who gives this woman to be the bride?"

Isaiah said, "Me and her mother."

He then went to stand in the back of the room with Barbara and the others. Charlie held out his hands to Frankie as she came to him. They held hands and smiled at each other as if they were the only ones in the world.

Charlie whispered, "You are the purtiest thing I have seen in all my born days."

The preacher cleared his throat twice in order to get Charlie's attention from his deep admiration of Frankie. "Is there anyone here who knows why this marriage should not take place?" He paused for a moment. "If not then let's proceed. Do you, Frankie Stuart, take this man, Charles Silver, to be your lawful wedded husband?"

Frankie said softly, "I do."

"Do you, Charles Silver, take Frankie Stuart to be your lawful wedded wife?"

"I do," came Charlie's sincere response.

Preacher Thomas performed the ceremony and closed by saying, "What God has joined together, let no man put asunder. I now pronounce you husband and wife. Charlie, you may now kiss your bride!"'

Everyone applauded as the couple kissed. Then Preacher Thomas reached out his hand to the couple and congratulated them. He told them he would continue to seek God's blessings for their marriage. He also told them he expected to see them both in church next Sunday morning. Both families crowded around the newlyweds with much ado and gave their approval and blessings.

Mrs. Stuart announced loudly, "Okay, everyone, I have made a big walnut cake, and we will serve it now."

The children, hungry and filled with excitement, could not wait for Frankie and Charlie to cut the cake. Aunt Bertha helped Barbara serve it. Barbara gave the children some apple juice to drink with their cake.

As the celebration gradually wound down, the two finally made their way outside and down the steps to Charlie's buggy. Everyone threw handfuls of rye on them for good luck and to help make their marriage a fruitful one.

Charlie helped Frankie into the buggy and then went back to the porch to help Blackston take the last of the things Frankie had packed. Neighbors and family had also packed canned vegetables, flour, cornmeal, and other items for their home and placed them in the buggy. While this was going on, Al slipped over with some old pots and pans and tied them to the rear of the buggy. When it turned and headed up the mountain, the sound of the best wishes, along with the pots and pans rattling along in the gravel, made old Dan a bit jumpy. As they pulled away, he stepped lively. Frankie looked back and waved good-bye to her folks, who were standing on the porch with the Silver family.

Chapter Four

The trip went quickly. The last rays of the sun were just going down behind the mountain as the two arrived in their little cove. Charlie had worked so hard to build their new home, and he hoped Frankie would be happy with it. He could not wait for her to see the little house.

When Frankie first saw it, she grabbed Charlie and gave him a warm hug and kiss that caused him to drop the reins.

"Charlie, the house is beautiful. It looks so nice."

He told her to close her eyes. This was the moment for which they had been waiting a long time. They pulled up in the yard. Charlie lifted her from the buggy and pushed open the door with his foot. "Now, don't peek."

When he put her down, she opened her eyes. She looked around and then threw her arms around Charlie's broad, strong shoulders again and said, "It's even nicer than I imagined. You have worked so hard, and it is so lovely."

Charlie went outside to the buggy and brought Frankie's things inside for her. Frankie then began to unpack.

Charlie looked at her and said, "I'm going to put old Dan in the shed before it gets any darker. Someday I'd like to build him a barn so we can have a place for him and a cow of our own. I'll just wait till tomorrow to take Dad's buggy back home. I'll be back in a few minutes."

They both were so excited and could not believe their time alone together had finally come. The neighboring ladies and Nancy had prepared a meal and covered it with a pretty tablecloth. Frankie and Charlie removed the cloth and had their first meal in their new home.

The ladies had also left a lot of can goods, a dough tray, rolling pin and wooden spoons made by their husbands. "We really do have a lot of good neighbors and friends," Frankie said as she looked at what they had left in the house for them.

Charlie responded, "They have left us a passel of things."

Later, as the two blew out the light and got into bed, all kinds of creepy noises began coming from around the house. Charlie sprang up and grabbed his pants and his rifle, which was hanging over the cabin door. Opening the door he spotted his brother, Al, and three or four of his friends in the moonlit shadows beating pans, shooting guns, and making all kinds of creepy noises.

Charlie lowered his gun and began to laugh. "Okay, fellas, that's enough! Thanks for the serenade. That's enough lollygagging around here."

He was still laughing as he went back inside. Frankie was sitting in bed holding the quilt under her chin. She was reaching for the nightgown and nightcap that she had placed at the foot of the bed.

"What in the world is going on out there? It sure sounds terrible."

"It's just Al and Josh and some of his buddies cuttin' up. They are just having fun. Don't let them scare you. I have participated in many such doin's for young married couples on their honeymoons. So I don't think I can blame my brother and his friends for doing the same for us."

The tumult soon died out. Charlie put his gun back over the door. He barred the door and pulled in the latch string.

Frankie slid back into the bed. Charlie quickly slipped out of his clothes and lunged into bed beside her. Their warm, naked bodies touched, and the long night of passion and pleasure completed their long-awaited, God-given urge to become one.

Their souls were now bonded forever. This crescendo ended with both totally consumed. Charlie was soon asleep almost to unconsciousness. Frankie lay beside him with her arm across his waist and her head on his chest. She kept listening to every heartbeat until she also fell asleep.

Charlie awoke when Frankie, dressed in her nightgown, pounced on top of him and began smothering him with kisses. "Honey, are you gonna sleep all day? Your breakfast is ready."

"Forget the breakfast," Charlie said, trying to get awake. He pulled her down to him. He then pushed the covers from under her. They found themselves again in another fit of sensual passion and love. They lay beside each other for a long time, enjoying a happiness that was totally new to both of them.

"I hope this never ends. You are very wonderful. I love you, Frankie, with all my heart and soul."

"I love you too, Charlie. You are all I need. Your breakfast is cold. I'll warm it up for you."

"I don't mind my breakfast being cold. You've warmed me up."

Charlie pulled on his pants and opened the cabin door. He stood stretching as the bright, warm sunshine struck his bare chest. He felt as if he had conquered the whole world.

Frankie had rekindled the fire, and the smell of food got his attention. This would be their first meal Frankie had prepared in their new home. Charlie pulled her away from the cooking and gave her a long kiss and hug. There was the tantalizing aroma of biscuits baking in the small Dutch oven that she had heaped with hot coals. Soon the smell of side meat also filled the small room.

This was the happiest moment of Charlie's life. He got the wooden bucket, dashed out to the spring, and carried in cold water along with a pitcher of cold milk Al had left for them in their new spring box. Charlie placed them on a table in the corner. After the two ate their breakfast together, he knew he had found a good cook—and a beautiful one as well.

That night they sat down to a wonderful supper of crackling cornbread and milk with stewed potatoes.

Charlie ate his fill and said, "I feel as if I'm gonna pop."

On Sunday Charlie suggested they attend church.

Frankie replied, "Well, at our weddin', didn't we promise Preacher Thomas we'd go?"

"Not really, but he did ask us. Maybe we should go. It is his day to preach."

After they had their baths and were dressed for church, the sound of the church bell could be heard coming from the top of the hill.

"We'd better git a move on if we don't want to be late," Frankie told Charlie.

"I'm hurrying as fast as I can. You know, I don't mind church. Do you remember me watching you sing in the choir at your church?"

"Oh hush, and come on. We're gonna be late, and I don't want everyone gawking at us as we go in."

They hurried out the door. They held hands as they went down the road and around the curve to the church. There was already a small group of people gathered.

They were greeted by Charlie's mom and dad and the rest of the family. Each child gave Charlie and Frankie a big hug except Al, who hugged only Frankie. When they all got inside, Lucinda asked her mom if she could sit beside Frankie as the rest of the eight children filed into their regular pew. Nancy nodded her approval. Lucinda sat beside Frankie and leaned up against her like a purring cat. Frankie put her arm around her.

Lucinda looked up and whispered, "You are so beautiful."

Frankie whispered back, "Thank you. You are too."

Mrs. Silver gave Lucinda that look that said without words, "No talking in church."

The preacher was shaking hands and welcoming everyone. He went over to Charlie and Frankie and said, "I am glad to see you folks. How are you enjoying married life?"

"Fine. Just fine, Preacher," Charlie answered. "We should have gotten ourselves married sooner. I like married life."

"Oh, y'all are still on your honeymoon. I hope it will last a long time. Frankie, it is good to have you at our service today. Who is this young lady beside you?"

"This is my little girl. Don't you think she is pretty?"

"Pretty is as pretty does. I think she looks like her big brother." He patted her on the head and made his way to the pulpit. "Everyone who will come sing in the choir, come on up," he announced.

Some people got up and went to the choirloft.

Charlie asked Frankie, "Why don't you go help them sing? You have a pretty voice. You'll know all the old hymns."

"No, not now. I might go help them later. I would rather stay here with you and Lucinda. I'd like to get used to going to church here first, if you don't mind."

The choir sang "Rock of Ages" and "Bringing in the Sheaves" a cappella from the old, worn hymnals.

Preacher Thomas announced, "It is time to take up the offering."

Charlie was glad he'd taken several coins from the beautiful sugar bowl on the mantle where they kept their money. Frankie's mother had given the bowl to her. Several deacons passed the plates. They reached out and shook hands with Charlie and Frankie as they passed the offering plates.

After the collection was taken, the preacher asked Lula Grant to come sing a special song: "I'm Glad Somebody Prayed for Me." It had many verses, and at times she spoke them instead of singing. At times it sounded as if she made it up as she went. When she finished there was a thunder of "amens" and "praise the Lords."

After she was seated, Preacher Thomas said, "Everyone turn in your Bibles to Romans chapter three and verse twenty-three."

Mrs. Silver handed her Bible to Charlie and Frankie.

"Let's stand together for the reading of God's Holy word," said the preacher. "For all have sinned and come short of the glory of God. You may be seated."

Charlie had been going to church here as long as he could recollect, but now he had a wife and did not feel alone. He felt like a man.

Preacher Thomas began his sermon. "These scriptures tell us that all have sinned and come short of the glory of God. That *all* includes me and every one of you. We are all sinners by choice and bound for hell if we do not turn to Jesus Christ.

"Now, look on down in chapter six, verse twenty-three. It says, 'For the wages of sin is death; but the gift of God is eternal life through Jesus Christ our Lord.' God has provided a way for us to go to heaven. That is Jesus Christ our Lord. Then, in chapter ten and verse nine, we read, 'That if thou shalt confess with thy mouth the Lord Jesus and shalt believe in thine heart that God hath raised him from the dead, thou shalt be saved.' This scripture does not say you can be good enough to go to heaven. It doesn't say you can work your way into heaven. All of this tells you that you must believe God raised Jesus from the grave, and you can be saved."

Several people in the congregation hollered, "Amen!"

"You must repent of your sins and turn from your wicked ways. Have you done that, my friend? If not, today is the day of salvation. He is a God of forgiveness. I am going to ask the song leader to lead us in an invitation hymn."

The song began. Charlie reached his hand out to Frankie, and they both went to the front and knelt in prayer. The preacher joined them, and several others gathered around them and prayed loudly.

Pastor Thomas whispered to Charlie, "Are you saved?" He did not wait for an answer. "If not ask for His forgiveness and invite Him into your heart, and He will save you. Are you saved, Frankie? If not just repent and accept Jesus." The preacher stood and said, "Let's continue singing and praying as these two pray through."

The praying got louder as everyone called on God to save these two precious sinners. Finally Frankie and Charlie stood and hugged one another as the others crowded around them.

The preacher said, "Have you made things right with the Lord?"

They both answered, "Yes."

Jacob and Nancy came up and hugged them, and they all made their way back to their seats.

The preacher dismissed his little flock with a long, laborious prayer while he made his way to the back door. He shook hands with everyone as they filed out of the little church. Most of the small congregation stood talking with one another for a long time in the churchyard. This was an important part of the service for these mountain people. They talked as the children played and chased one another outside. The Silver family started to leave and asked Frankie and Charlie to go home with them for Sunday dinner.

Charlie said, "Maybe next time. We will just go home. Frankie has fixed some dinner for us. Thanks for the invite, though, Mom."

Lucinda went to her mom and asked, "May I go home with them, Mama?"

"Honey, mind your manners. You are supposed to be invited first. They haven't asked you over."

Frankie heard this and went over to Mrs. Silver. "That's all right. She is welcome to come home with us. We will walk her back home this evening after dinner."

Lucinda, Frankie, and Charlie made their way home. Frankie cooked some potatoes and corncakes. As it was Sunday, she had cooked a pot of venison stew and left it hanging in the fireplace to keep it warm. Charlie had picked some branch lettuce, and Frankie poured hot side-meat grease that was left over from breakfast on it to wilt it. Lucinda, Charlie, and Frankie enjoyed their Sunday dinner together. Lucinda then helped Frankie do the dishes.

Later that afternoon there was a knock at the door. When Charlie went to answer, it he found Al standing outside. Charlie invited his brother in. Al spoke to Frankie, and then the two brothers sat and talked while Lucinda and Frankie finished the dishes.

Al told him, "I miss you now that you are married, but I do have more room in our bed now that you are gone." They both laugh. "I'd like to see you more. You've turned out to be an old, ornery married man. I miss the old Charlie. Maybe we could go coon hunting again before long."

Charlie responded, "I miss you too, Al, but I am happy here with Frankie."

"I came over to see you and walk Lucinda home. Mom said you two might like to be alone on such a pretty Sunday evening."

Al left with his sister, and Charlie and Frankie were alone again.

She told him, "I enjoyed her visit. It is fun having children around. I'd like to have some of our own someday. Do you want to have children, Charlie?"

"I don't know what it would be like without them. I have so many brothers and sisters, but I would like to have some of our own."

The following Sunday Preacher Thomas asked Frankie and Charlie if they would like to be baptized.

"We have several others who have made professions of their faith, and we will be baptizing them next Sunday evening," he told them.

After another "hell's hot and heaven's sweet" message, the preacher ended by saying, "Just a reminder: there will be a baptism next Sunday at three o'clock down at the river. It will be held at the regular place—the boys' old swimming hole. We have five candidates who will be baptized."

After the service Nancy told Frankie she would make her a heavy gown to wear for the baptism.

"I'm really afraid to be baptized," Frankie confided in Charlie on their way home. "I can't swim. What if he drowns me?"

"Honey, don't be afraid. I'll be on one side of you and the preacher on the other. I will make sure you are all right."

The Sunday afternoon of the baptism arrived, and Frankie was still dreading the water. She and Charlie made their way down to the river. When they got there, a small crowd had already gathered on the bank, including Isaiah and Barbara. The pastor lifted his hands to hush the congregation.

"Let us pray. Lord, thank you for these five souls who have turned their lives over to you. Thank you that they are outwardly showing they are following you. Bless everyone here. Amen. Let's sing 'Shall We Gather at the River.'"

As they started singing, he began wading out into the water. "We will start with the children first," he told them and reached his hand out to the first girl, who looked scared. He placed his other hand in the air and said, "Buried in Christ Jesus and raised to a newness of life." He put his hand over the child's nose and mouth and then laid her down in the water and quickly raised her out. There was a chorus of "amens," "hallelujahs," and "praise the Lord" from the onlookers as the child came up out of the water. This continued for the other three children until it was Frankie and Charlie's turn. Charlie took Frankie by the hand and gently led her out into the water to Preacher Thomas, who was waiting for them.

"I'd like to say how thankful I am this young couple are starting off their home life together in the right way. I am glad they want to serve the Lord. A home without the Lord is just a house."

He baptized Frankie, who was trembling due to nerves and the cold water. Charlie helped her out of the river and to his mother, who was waiting with a towel. Charlie went back and was submerged in the stream where he and his brother, Al, had baptized each other many times while swimming. There was another chorus of "hallelujah" and "praise the Lord" as he came to shore.

The small congregation dispersed, making their way back into the hills and mountains. The wet couple straggled along on their way back home.

Frankie said, "Thanks for being there beside me, Charlie."

Weeks and months went by. The couple was as happy as they had been the day they had gotten married. They rarely went anywhere except over the mountain to visit at Charlie's father's house. Sometimes while Charlie was helping his father split rails or shingles, Frankie spent the day with Mrs. Silver.

Occasionally Frankie's folks would load up in their wagon and come over to visit with her. Frankie enjoyed these short visits and always looked forward to her parents' return. Frankie and Charlie were happy and content.

More happiness came their way when Frankie announced to Charlie that he was going to be a father. Charlie was so excited he did not know how to respond; after all he had never been a father before.

"We're gonna have a child of our own? You mean I'm going to be a papa? Well, don't worry or fret, I will do all the heavy chores. You just take care of yourself and the baby."

Charlie was extremely careful not to let Frankie lift heavy pots or the water buckets. He did not let her carry in any wood or even place some on the fire. He made every effort to take care of all her needs.

Meanwhile Charlie and his dad were making a beautiful cradle for the baby. When they finished it, they set it near the fireplace with new covers made by Frankie and Mrs. Silver. The whole family could not wait for the new arrival. Time seemed to drag on, almost as it had when Charlie was waiting to marry Frankie. Everyone was waiting patiently for the big day.

Finally one afternoon Frankie called frantically to Charlie, who was working outside. "Go fetch your mama! I believe the baby's on its way!"

Charlie ran to the top of the ridge as fast as his legs would take him and shouted as loud as he could, "Mama, we need you. I think we're going to have a baby!"

His mother was hanging out her washing on the garden fence and responded by dropping the clothes and shouting back, "Fetch some water and put it on the fire to heat. I'll be there as soon as I can! I need to go inside to tell Jacob so he can go get Mrs. Wilson. I need to tell the others and get some things before I come!"

Charlie raced back down the ridge to Frankie. He checked on her and then went to the spring to get the water. He poured it in the big, black kettle and hung it in the fireplace to heat. He then placed more wood on the fire.

It was not long till Charlie's mother arrived and told him Jacob had gone to get Mrs. Wilson. She was known throughout the area as the best midwife one could find anywhere.

"They will not be long, based on the pace Jacob took as he left with the wagon!" Nancy told them.

Charlie paced back and forth until Jacob arrived. Mrs. Lee Anna Wilson was a fat woman with graying hair braided around her head. She had age furrows across her weathered face. She was a talkative and outright pushy woman. She entered the cabin and gave Charlie a stern look as she placed a sack on the table. She flapped her apron at him.

"Get outside, young man. We will not be needing you in here. We women can take care of everything just fine. You've already done your job! If it hadn't been fer you, we'd not be having to do this. I'll call you if I need you. Now skedaddle out of here!"

Charlie obeyed and went outside. His mother closed the door behind him. Again he began to pace back and forth in front of the door.

Jacob interrupted him. "Now, son, I remember doing the same thing you're doing once or twice, but I certainly did not do it all nine times. I soon realized I was not helping a dab by wearing out the soles of my old boots. Just have a seat and wait. It probably won't be long."

Charlie nervously asked his father, "Dad, what if the same thing happens to Frankie that happened to my mama when I was born? What will I do?"

"Oh, Charlie, don't worry about that happening. It doesn't happen very often. Frankie is in good hands. Besides, there are many prayers being sent up for her. Mrs. Wilson is not just a good midwife—she is also known all over for her remedies for any kind of sickness. She has set up with many a sick person who was bad off till they got better or died."

"Where did she learn all this?"

"Well, part of it has been handed down for generations in her family. She also knows an old Indian who lives over on Crooked Creek by the name of Two Trees. He is a medicine man."

"Dad, that's amazing. It must be great to help someone who is doing poorly."

"She doctored your grandpa, George, when he was down in his back. I have learned a lot from her myself. One time I had a serious cut from a cross-cut saw on my knee, and it wouldn't heal. She told me to go to the big Roan Mountain, prick the blisters on a balsam tree, and collect the turpentine and put it on my cut. It healed in no time. She has a special tree in her yard called a slippery elm, and people come from miles around just to get some bark of it for medicine.

She makes poultices out of it for doctoring. Once, when you were very small, she told me to give you juice from a baked onion for your cold, and it worked."

"I don't remember that."

"No, you were knee high to a grasshopper when that happened. She is even good at doctoring animals. Once the best horse I ever had stepped on an axe, and it swung around and cut her leg pretty bad. The horses name was Maude. She had a white star on her forehead and a set of white socks."

"Is she the one you used to tell me about that would stick her head out the window and whinny for you when it was time to feed her?"

"Yes. Anyway Mrs. Wilson wrapped her leg in turpentine, pine rosin, and some other stuff. The horse got well and plowed many a row of corn after that."

Time dragged on, and they began talking about hunting and fishing. They laughed about the time when Jacob had shot Tom in the leg while hunting.

"I thought I had killed Tom for sure. Boy, I sure was relieved to find it was not so bad."

Jacob stopped whittling the baby toy he was making and started nodding off to sleep.

Suddenly something sweeter than the sound of the music Charlie loved so much struck his ears, and he broke out in goose bumps. It was the sound of his child's first cry. This was so beautiful now, but eventually it would not be as welcome in the middle of the night. For now there could be nothing more thrilling. He jumped to his feet to face the door when his mother opened it.

She calmly put her arm around him. "You are a daddy, Charlie. You may come in now."

Charlie looked at his mother's face and asked anxiously, "Is Frankie all right?"

His mother nodded and smiled as he rushed around her to Frankie's bedside.

Frankie whispered with a weak and tired voice, "We have a beautiful daughter."

Charlie took her hand and, with a lusty, nervous, grin said, "Thank you. I'm sure she will grow up to be as pretty and as smart as her mother. I am the proudest papa in the whole world."

Charlie's mother and the midwife had been working with the baby, and now Mrs. Wilson handed her to Frankie, who pulled her close and began to nurse.

After cleaning up the house and telling Nancy good-bye, the midwife announced to Frankie and Charlie, "Well, I have done what I came to do. Congratulations on your baby. I'd better git home and fix supper for my man."

Jacob and Mrs. Wilson headed down the narrow road toward her home.

"I believe Charlie was as nervous as I was when he was born," Jacob told Mrs. Wilson.

"I don't understand why it seems to bother you men so much. You're not the ones doing the hard work. You have fun, and then we women pay the price."

They both laughed as they continued on down the road.

"Yes, I forgot, I know it was a sad time for you when your first wife passed away giving birth to Charlie," Mrs. Wilson grunted as an afterthought. "It shocked us all," she finished with a tremor in her voice.

Nancy told Frankie and Charlie that she would remain a little while longer before she went home to prepare supper for Jacob and the children. "It won't take long because I asked Margaret to start supper if I am not back in time and told the kids to have their chores all done. I will bring y'all back some supper."

"I know they are dying to see the baby," Frankie told Nancy.

"Yes, I know they are, so I'll bring them back with me to see her if that's all right with you."

Frankie and Charlie discussed their new arrival after everyone left. Frankie held her out for Charlie to take.

"I don't know how to hold a little bitty baby. I might hurt her."

"Now, take her. You'll soon get used to it."

Charlie was tenderly and awkwardly rocking the baby and had even decided it was not so hard after all when Mrs. Silver knocked on the door. He handed the baby to Frankie and opened the door for his mother. There were a lot of gawking faces peering in from behind her.

She placed a basket of food on the table as she said, "I brought you some venison stew. I hope you like it. I put a lot of hot pepper in it. I know you like it hot."

"Thanks, Mom."

"They are all so excited to see the baby. I told the children they could only come in one at a time to see her. Is that okay with you, Frankie?"

"That will be fine. Charlie, will you move a chair over here by the bed for them?"

They filed in one at a time and sat briefly looking at their new niece.

Finally Lucinda asked, "What are you going to name her? I like Daisy."

"We have not completely decided yet, but we have a good idea. As soon as we decide, we will let you know, okay?"

When the last child had filed out, Nancy announced, "Children, we had better git going for home. We don't want to wear Frankie and the baby to a frazzle, do we? Do I need to stay with y'all tonight, Charlie? I will set up with her if I need to."

"No, we will be all right."

"I'll be glad to set with her and take care of the baby if you'ns need me."

"No, Mom, you've done enough. I'll come after you if I need you. I would like it if you would stay with them awhile tomorrow, though. I want to go tell Frankie's mom and dad about the baby and invite them to come see her."

"Well, I'll be back early tomorrow to check on you both, okay? I hope Margaret gets those black walnuts cracked out so I can bake us a cake. If she does I will bring you both some when I come back tomorrow."

There was a chorus of "bye" from outside the open door as the family left for home.

Frankie and Charlie were so happy and grateful to God that their baby girl was strong and normal. Their thoughts then turned to naming her, and together they decided to call her Nancy, after Charlie's mother.

As each day passed, Charlie insisted little Nancy looked more and more like her mother, which Frankie would counter by saying, "I think she favors her dad."

Charlie liked holding Nancy and getting her to smile. He enjoyed rocking her to sleep while Frankie continued to rest. It was hard to find a happier couple than this little young family tucked away in this tiny mountainous cove.

Chapter Five

Charlie took care of the cooking and even put out wash while Frankie was regaining her strength. He made sure the baby and Frankie both were taken care of as well as possible. When little Nancy woke them crying in the middle of the night, Charlie got up and rocked her until peace prevailed once again. He still was not too good at changing a diaper, although he seemed to be getting better at it with plenty of practice. Frankie laughed and teased him about being a good mom but often told him how much she appreciated the attention he was giving them.

Soon Frankie was up and doing her household chores again, and Charlie was able to spend more time at work around the house. He often went over to help his father. They had a load of chestnut bark ready to haul down to Morganton to be used at a tannery. They both had several deer, muskrat, mink and cow hides they planned to sell while there. The job of taking the bark and hides fell on Charlie and Al because his father had to stay and work in the fields. The trip was about sixty miles and would take the oxen about two days and nights to make the trip there and back. They planned to sleep under the wagon in Morganton before heading back home.

Frankie told Charlie, "I'm afraid to stay here by myself, especially at night."

So Charlie asked his sister, Margaret, to come stay with her. This was the first time Charlie had been away from his family for any length of time, especially overnight. Occasionally he had gone coon hunting with Joshua or Al.

When he returned he was so glad to see Frankie and Nancy. He kept telling Frankie how much he had missed her and how much

Nancy had grown while he was gone. Charlie had bought Frankie a lovely silk dress from the dry-goods store in Morganton. He couldn't wait to surprise her with it.

When she unwrapped the dress, she was so excited and surprised. Frankie could not wait to put it on. She told Charlie as she planted a kiss on his cheek, "It is the first store-bought dress I have ever had. Thank you so much."

Frankie put the new dress on, and she and Charlie ate supper together. Afterward they wrapped Nancy in a blanket and went for a walk down toward the river. It was a beautiful fall day, and the chill of winter could barely be felt in the air.

While they walked Charlie said, "Grandpa George always says when the goldenrod is blooming, it is only six weeks till frost."

Frankie replied as she looked up at the sky, "Well, my grandmother always told us red clouds in the morning is sailor's fair warning, red clouds at night is sailor's delight. The sky is very beautiful. It looks like red and gold dust being spilled over the mountaintops."

Charlie also looked up. "That is a beautiful sunset with those red and gold clouds. I think about my mom and heaven when I see them."

Frankie was still looking at the sunset. "When Mama talks about the weather, she always says you can count the stars in a circle around the moon, and that's how many days till falling weather. I guess we'd better take warning. Charlie, have you ever wondered where old folks come up with some of these sayings?"

"I don't know, but I believe some of them are true. I guess they have learned to observe nature better than we do."

They both laughed as they continued their walk down to the large, granite rock at the swimming hole. They walked out on the huge rock and sat and talked while Charlie held little Nancy.

Charlie whispered to Frankie, "What a beautiful and peaceful place to spend a quiet evening with my family. I am so glad to be back home."

Sometimes they would go to the church Frankie's parents attended. They went on Decoration Day with her parents. Frankie enjoyed the day. She told Charlie on the way back home, "I'm going to write a poem about the good time I had at church today."

The next day after supper, she asked Charlie if he would like to hear her new poem.

Charlie said, "I'll hold the baby while you read it."

"I call it 'Decoration Day,'" Frankie said, then recited:

> Once every year there was a very
> Special Sunday event.
> It was called Decoration Day
> By all those who went.
> Mom and Aunt Bertha
> Made crepe-paper roses dipped in wax
> And wreaths of Galax and dog hobble
> To complete the batch.
> Mom's dinner of fried chicken
> And stack cake
> Was packed and ready to take.
> We donned our Sunday best
> So filled with starch
> They felt as if they'd break.
> We loaded the dinner along with the flowers
> On Dad's old wagon
> And arrived safely without spilling the dinner—
> With God's help, and that's not braggin'.
> The church was big and beautiful
> With its steeple standing pale against the sky.
> People were already placing flowers
> On graves in the cemetery nearby.
> Mom and I placed flowers on the graves
> Of my grandparents, who I never knew

And some on the tiny grave
Of Aunt Bertha's baby too.
We went to the preaching, where everyone gone
before
Was named, revered, and loved
As my stomach growled louder and louder.
Seemed like he'd preach 'till we'd all gone above.
Finally, with a hymn and the last amen said
We headed outside under the huge oaks
To a glorious spread.
One of the deacons asked God's blessings
On all the food.
Someone said quietly, "Dig in."
And that changed the mood.
All the food and desserts were wonderful to see
But the best thing there
Was to have you beside me.
The day finished with fellowship
And gospel singing.
We all left not knowing
What the next year would be bringing.
Like the familiar epitaph
On many of the stones of those passed away
"Gone but not forgotten"
Are all those precious days.

"Well, do you like it?" Frankie asked.

"Like it? No, I love it," Charlie replied.

"Well, it just tells the way I felt."

"I would like it if you'd read it to Mom and Dad someday. You are a good poet. I need to buy you a new tablet to write your poems in. The next time I go to Morganton, I will get you one."

"Thanks. I'll write another for you someday. I'd like to write one about you and little Nancy."

As the Indian summer approached and the radiant colors of fall arrived across the vast, rugged mountain slopes, Nancy grew and was more lovely and responsive with each passing day. Frankie and Charlie were both extremely proud of her. She started to notice the world around her. Charlie spent more and more time with her. He enjoyed watching her playful antics. He loved making faces at her just to see her sweet smile. She was about nine months old now and enjoyed being cuddled in her dad's strong and loving arms.

Charlie was still helping his father with stacking the last field of hay and making fodder shocks to feed the cows and horses for the coming winter. He helped Jacob gather the corn and put it in the crib. They hauled several wagonloads and pitched it up into the barn loft for the cows and horses. They also made several haystacks in the field.

Jacob told Charlie, "I plan to give you some feed for old Dan and your new flock of chickens this winter."

Fall was an ideal time to hunt, and Charlie began taking advantage of every opportunity to head out to the woods. He loved to see the brilliant colors as the trees changed and their leaves started to fall. He killed some pheasants and a grouse for his family's table. He also killed several deer and bears. He always divided the large game with his Mom and Dad. Several times he came home with a load of fresh hog meat after killing a wild boar. He also shared this with Nancy and Jacob. But more often he came in empty handed after spending all day in the woods.

He also was spending more time over at his Mom and Dad's place, leaving Frankie alone all day with Nancy there in the hollow.

Frankie complained, "I don't like being shut up in this little house every day in this lonesome holler! All I do is carry in the wood, cook, and tend to the baby."

Charlie didn't respond to her. He only made matters worse by avoiding confrontation and not saying a word. He increasingly was away even more.

He finally told her, "I am spending more time over at the store where men gather around the pot-bellied stove and tell yarns. What's wrong with that? They have their crops all laid by, and most of their work is all done for winter."

Charlie loved to hear the tales that had been handed down for generations about hunting and fights with the Indians. It did not take long for him to realize that even if some of the stories were exaggerated, these men were still real brave frontiersmen.

The weather continued to get worse as winter approached. Charlie started worrying about his family. He wondered if they would be able to survive the winter. What if sickness came, or what if they did not have enough food to sustain them during the cold months? The more he thought about these things, his worries seemed to multiply. This was the first year he would be responsible for a family of his own.

He told Frankie, "I think I should go look for work at one of the mines or at Sam Gouge's sawmill."

Frankie told him, "We will get by with the help of both our families. You don't need to find work."

"This is not what I want. I don't want my family just to get by. Frankie, I don't want to depend on our folks either. Besides, they have done enough for us already. Mom and Dad have a lot of mouths to feed."

This notion of a job was unusual since most people in the area did not depend upon an outside source of income. Most of the mountain people were almost entirely self-sufficient. They depended on the crops and what they could produce on the mountain slopes. They barely ever needed to purchase anything from stores to sustain them. What they did purchase was some salt and soda to be used in the kitchen for making bread and seasoning.

Money was very scarce, and there was not much a person could do to earn any. The mountain women dried and preserved enough vegetables and fruits to last till the next season. Frankie had not been able to preserve much food. Their little garden spot had not produced well as they'd put it out late in the season. Charlie's mom had helped them by sharing from her and Jacob's fields and garden, but Charlie realized that times could get tough if they happened to have a harsh winter.

Between hunting and claiming to be looking for some work, Charlie was getting used to spending more and more time away from his little family. Frankie began to wonder where he was during all these unexplained absences. Sometimes he came home drinking. She hounded him about loafing for the biggest part of the day. Sometimes he returned late at night. It seemed he did not want to be with her and Nancy even when he did return. The strangest thing about the entire ordeal to Frankie was that he didn't want to tell her where he had been or where he was going when he left.

Sometimes he would simply tell her, "I'm going down to the store to catch up on the latest news." Frankie could not understand the drastic change that had come over him. At first she wondered why he was spending so much of his time at the store. He was neglecting his work around the house. He didn't even offer to bring in the wood or water anymore.

One day she decided to check on Charlie because he had said he was spending so much of his time down at the store. A neighbor passed by with a sack of corn across the back of his mule. He was taking it to the mill beside the general store to be ground.

Frankie stopped him and asked, "I see you are taking a turn of corn to the mill next to the store. Will you look for Charlie at the store and tell him to bring me a box of soda when he comes home?" She'd asked this so neither party would suspect anything. Later that same afternoon, the neighbor returned with his ground corn.

He reported to Frankie, "I am sorry, but I was unable to find Charlie at the store. I brought you a box of soda. It cost a nickel."

She got a nickel from the sugar bowl on the mantle, paid him, and thanked him as he rode away. Now she had a real reason for letting her suspicion be aroused. She did not know what to do about asking Charlie where he had been as he always got extremely put out with her if she did. As she prepared supper, she wondered why he had told her he was going to the store when he was not there.

Frankie could not understand what was going on and knew it was not like Charlie to behave like this. She did not dare to talk to his folks about it because it would only make matters worse if he found out. As she put the plates on the table and occasionally looked out the door for Charlie, she thought, *Perhaps he will tell me where he has been today without me asking.*

Charlie returned late in the evening. Frankie waited for him to tell her where he had been. During their quiet supper, he did not mention it. She expected him to tell her while he played with Nancy after supper, but he did not volunteer any information. When they were getting ready for bed and there was still nothing, Frankie decided to question Charlie. She told him about having the neighbor look for him at the store.

Charlie jumped out of bed and shouted, "That makes me plumb mad. You don't trust me. Why are you checking up on me? I should beat the daylights out of you!" He grabbed her by the throat and said, "If you do something like that again, you will be sorry!" He told her he had left the store looking for work again.

Trembling, she pleadingly told him, "There is no need for you to continue looking for work, honey. We will manage without you finding a job."

It had been nearly a year now since they were married and Charlie carried her over the threshold of their new home. Frankie could not understand what had happened to that close feeling of devotion and love they once had as a new family. She wondered what had happened to him. He did not pay any attention to her like he once did. Frankie spent many long hours weeping her heart out. When Mrs. Silver or her family occasionally came to visit, she pretended everything was just fine.

Frankie tried to make herself think logically. Brooding over Charlie's obvious disregard for her feelings, she also let a coldness creep into what had been the warmest place in her life. It was not by choice, but she watched as the burning flame of love that she thought would never die slowly dimmed, and the darkness closed in around her.

Finally Frankie, bound up by her worries and fears, decided there was surely more to those absences than Charlie was willing to admit. Thinking about it she came to the awful conclusion that there must be another woman involved. After all he was good looking and was admired by all the other women. Thanks to a strong imagination, this woman became a reality to Frankie, who became so wrapped up in her suspicions she refused to speak to Charlie even when he occasionally tried to talk with her.

Now Charlie began to wonder what caused Frankie to act in such a sullen manner. Sometimes he threatened her and even acted like he was going to hit her. It made the divide between them even larger and more unbearable.

Charlie often took little Nancy from her cradle and played with her on the enormous bearskin rug by the spacious, open fireplace. Frankie sat and pretended to be perfectly content doing her mending and sewing.

Time dragged by, and Charlie was still spending a large amount of his time away from home. Now part of the reason for his absences was the coldness he found there. He was spending much of his time at the store and had started drinking more. He was not helping around the house with any of the chores. It was the middle of December, and there had been no change in their strained relationship. Frankie continued her distrustful suspicions and kept them all in her heart without letting anyone know the reason for her worry and frustration.

Chapter Six

Very early on the snowy morning of December 23, Frankie and her young daughter went to visit Mrs. Silver. As they trudged down the snow-covered hillside, Frankie noticed that Mrs. Silver had built a fire under the big, black wash pot. She was preparing to do the family wash. Mrs. Silver stirred the fire under the steaming pot as the water came to a rolling boil. She noticed Frankie with Nancy in her arms coming through the fresh, deep snow. After making a few more whacks with her wash paddle, she laid it down on her weathered wash bench. She hurriedly dried her hands on her worn and ragged apron as she rushed over to meet the cold travelers.

"Morning, Mrs. Silver," Frankie said with a trembling voice.

"Morning, Frankie. Aren't you two nearly frozen half to death? I am glad to see you. We haven't seen you in several days. But it's awful early to be out on a nippy morning like this! I should have known better than to try to do my wash today." She reached for the baby, took her in her arms, and said, "Let's go inside and warm up. I'll finish my washing after a while. Like I said it's almost too cold to wash today anyway. We don't want the baby to freeze out here in this snow."

"Oh, my washing is already done, and I've even scoured the floor and cleaned the house," Frankie said.

"My goodness, girl, I didn't know I have such a smart and power-ful daughter-in-law. You surely got up early to do a day's work before dawn! Come on in, honey child. You must be half frozen to a whicker pucker."

Once they were inside, Nancy could see something was troubling Frankie. She broke the silence by asking, "Why didn't Charlie come with you? I hope you didn't leave that lazy young'n in bed after you did all that passel of work this morning. You look a little peaked. Are you ailing, child?"

"That's the reason I came!" Frankie said with a troubled voice. "Charlie left yesterday saying he was going over to George Young's place to get some Christmas liquor. He hasn't come back yet. I waited up for him late last night. I got up early and did my wash and scouring while I waited and looked for him to come home this morning."

As she talked big tears began to form in her eyes, and she wrung her hands. Mrs. Silver put Nancy down on the bed. She then placed her arms around Frankie, trying to console her.

"Now, now, child. There is no need to be so upset, sweetie," Nancy said in her quiet, consoling tone.

"I'm terribly worried about him" came Frankie's trembling reply. "What if he fell through the ice while he was trying to cross the river? Please help me. I don't know what to do. It's just not like my Charlie to go off and stay away without me knowing where he is, especially if he is going to be gone at night. I believe something awful has happened to him. Would you please have Jacob and the boys go look for him?"

Mrs. Silver went out on the back porch and yelled loudly for Jacob, who was doing his early morning chores in the barn.

Jacob appeared outside the barn and asked, "Nancy, what do you want, honey?"

"Come inside, Pa. Frankie is here."

"Can I finish my feeding? I'll be there in a few minutes."

"No, you need to come in now."

Nancy went back in to check on Frankie. She was comforting her daughter-in-law and giving her words of encouragement when Jacob and Al entered the room. Al set his basket of eggs down and followed his dad. Jacob placed a fresh bucket of milk on the table and went to Frankie.

Jacob asked, "Frankie, what's wrong? Is something wrong with the baby? Where's Charlie? Why didn't he come with you?"

Frankie started to explain to them that Charlie had not come home last night.

"She is awful worried about him." Nancy helped Frankie explain that he had been gone overnight. This was not normal behavior for Charlie.

Jacob told Frankie with a consoling hug, "Now, honey, don't you worry so. He'll be all right. I am sure he'll be back sometime today. He may have spent the night at George Young's place because of the snow. We'll go look for him."

"Frankie, we might even meet him on his way home. He'll probably be home directly," Al said in a comforting and calm voice.

"As I said, if it will make you feel better, Al and I will go look for him."

"I'll jerk us up some breakfast before you go," Nancy said, turning toward the kitchen. Before long she had some side meat frying, and the aroma filled the house. This made Frankie sick to her stomach, and she had to go outside to get some fresh air.

When she returned Nancy asked, "Honey child, you're not expecting again, are you?"

"No, I don't think so. It's my nerves. I'm so upset over Charlie."

Jacob and Al gulped down some breakfast, but Frankie refused to eat. The men pulled on their winter wraps and went to the barn to get the horses. They decided to go to the cabin and see if Charlie had come home while Frankie had been gone. When they arrived, Al got down off his horse, poked his head in the cabin, and called for Charlie. There was no answer.

They continued their search by heading toward the river. Just below the cabin, they spotted what seemed to be faint boot prints in the glistening snow. Jacob got down off the horse to take a closer look. The blowing snow had drifted and almost filled the tracks. This was understandable since Frankie had told them Charlie had left early in the evening while it was still snowing. It had snowed most of the night. The tracks were extremely difficult to see but seemed to be headed for the river.

Jacob was leading his horse along behind him as he tried to follow the tracks in the deep snow. Al was still on his horse. They were getting closer to the river, and the tracks continued in that direction. The tracks went down to the crossing, which was completely frozen. The ice had a few inches of snow covering it. The tracks went a few feet out on the ice and suddenly stopped.

This troubled Jacob. He looked to Al and said, "They stop right there. Do you think he has fallen through the ice?"

"I can't see any breaks in the ice from here. Can you see anything from there, Pa?"

Jacob left Al and the horses and eased out onto the snow-covered ice. He carefully pushed the fallen snow away, but the stinging cold and bitter wind kept blowing it back. "No, I don't believe there is any sign of the ice being broken and freezing back," he said emphatically. "This is hard to understand. Maybe he was afraid to cross and turned back, but he would have had to step in the same tracks going back, wouldn't he?"

"Dad, maybe the ice is frozen back so smooth you can't tell," Al said as he got down from his horse.

Jacob was now worried that maybe Frankie was right. He kept telling himself not to let his imagination and worry get the best of him. He thought, *If Charlie has fallen through, it will be hard to find him. We might even have to wait weeks till the river thaws.* Jacob couldn't stand the thought of losing another member of his family. He had already had to give up one precious son, John, who died from a fever when he was just a child. He took a closer look and raked more snow away with his freezing hands to find what seemed to be cracks in the ice this time.

Jacob looked up at Al and said while searching his own mind for answers, "Maybe this is where he tested the ice and decided to turn back. Many times I have taken a rock and tossed it onto the ice to test it. It looks too small for a person to fall through into the river. Let's hope and pray that is what Charlie did."

"Dad, maybe he went farther downriver to cross. Maybe we should head that way to see if there are any more tracks in the snow."

They both turned from the river. Al led the horses along the bank as Jacob walked on ahead looking for tracks or any sign of Charlie. Jacob helped Al cross the river farther down and then sent him to George Young's place to look for Charlie.

Jacob said, "Stop at every house on the way back and ask if they have seen him. The storm was not too severe, but maybe he spent the night at someone's house after deciding it was too cold to try to make it home in this bone-chilling snow." Even as he said this, Jacob realized that if Charlie had spent the night, surely he would have made it home by now. And why had he not taken old Dan instead of walking?

It was almost noon. Jacob instructed Al to ask everyone he saw if they had seen Charlie at any time since his disappearance. Meanwhile Jacob began to check up and down the snow-covered river. He looked on both sides without finding any sign or tracks other than the ones they had found earlier leading down to the crossing. He continued his search around the banks of the river. He carefully uncovered snow mounds to see if Charlie had fallen in the snow and frozen. He had heard of fellows who got drunk and fell in the cold snow and had ended up freezing to death. These mounds proved to be only chunks of rotten wood or clumps of debris washed down by the river and deposited on the bank.

The sun was now rapidly disappearing behind the majestic, snow-covered Blue Ridge Mountains. It would soon be getting dark. Jacob was so cold and exhausted that he decided to head back home and wait for Al to return with some news. He would once again drop by Charlie's house to see if he had returned. He found the house still empty, so he grudgingly decided to head back home.

When he arrived he was met on the front porch by Nancy and all the children, along with Frankie. They were all asking questions at the same time and were eager for some news about Charlie. As they went inside, he told them Al had gone across the river to check if anyone had seen him lately. The children were getting upset and confused.

Nancy got them in a huddle and told them, "Let's all hold hands and pray. Dear God, we know that all things work together for the good of them who love you. We know you look after your sheep. And Lord, we pray you will take care of our Charlie and bring him safely back to us."

During the prayer Frankie began to tremble and weep. "I don't know what has happened to Charlie. I don't know what I can do without him!"

Mrs. Silver again consoled Frankie and assured her Al would probably come back with Charlie.

Jacob went to the fireplace to warm up when the prayer ended. Hours later, Al was heard outside as he returned and tied the horse reins to a post in the front yard. The whole family rushed out onto the front porch.

"Did you get any news from George or any of the neighbors?" Jacob asked as the whole family crowded around Al.

Frankie rushed forward, threw her arms around Al, and said with a trembling and broken voice, "You didn't find Charlie? I was hoping you'd find him and bring him back with you."

Al finally got a chance to say, "No, he has not been to George Young's. They have not seen him lately. None of the neighbors around have seen hide or hair of him." Al looked at his father and sadly asked, "What are we going to do, Dad?"

"I don't know, son. Let's all go inside where it's warm to talk."

The whole family, with their arms wrapped around one another, made their way back into the house. Jacob went to stand in front of the fire and said, "I really don't know what to do. Maybe I could go to some more neighbors' houses tonight and ask them to help us look for Charlie tomorrow." By this time the whole family was sobbing and making an effort to comfort one another.

"If I do that," Jacob went on, "at least we will have a head start tomorrow and have more than just the two of us looking. I'll go make my rounds. I'll probably be back late. Frankie, don't worry, honey. We'll find him."

Frankie sniffled as she spoke. "I don't know where else he could have gone. Do you have any idea where he would go, Al?"

"No, Frankie, I don't, but I'm sure he'll show up shortly. This is not like Charlie."

Nancy asked, "Frankie, why don't you go lie down with the baby and try to get some rest? Children, find something to do. I'll sit here and wait till your dad gets back. We need to have faith that God will take care of our Charlie. Maybe he'll show up before long."

"I'll go out to do the milking and feeding while you are gone, Pa. I'll also walk over and feed old Dan for Charlie. Is that okay?" Al said, trying to be helpful.

"That's good, Al. You have been a great help, son."

Nancy was still sitting in the rocking chair reading her Bible and praying when Jacob returned hours later. She occasionally got up and looked out and listened for Charlie's return. Jacob had contacted a good number of neighbors. They were going to come by and bring others with them at the break of dawn. Jacob was beat to a frazzle. He pulled a chair up to the fireplace and pulled off his wet boots to warm his cold feet. He began nodding as the fire burned down to embers.

Nancy continued to pray that God would give them strength and courage to stand in this hour of trial. Her thoughts turned to little Nancy. The baby needed her dad. Charlie's mother prayed that God would give them the wisdom to follow His will whatever it might be. She couldn't sleep because she was reminded of the bitter grief she and Jacob had felt as her other son had been laid to rest in an untimely grave from the fever. She asked faintly, "Lord, please don't let anything be wrong with my Charlie. Please bring him back to us."

As the first rays of light began to break over the cold mountains, Jacob got up and put another log on the fire. The coals were dying, so he stirred them to relight the flames. He found Nancy, with her Bible in her lap, asleep in the big rocker. He roused her, and she began preparing breakfast for the family.

She told Jacob and Al, "Don't worry about the milking and feeding. John and I will do it while you are gone. Rachel and Milton can carry in some wood for the fireplaces."

Al and his father went outside to meet the neighbors. They were prepared for a long day of searching.

One man said, "Jacob, we will be with you all day if that's what it takes."

Jacob was humbled that such a large group of friends and neighbors had gathered. The news of Charlie's absence had gotten around to many of them, and they were joining in the search.

The first group headed toward Charlie and Frankie's cabin to see if he had returned. When they discovered he was not up there, they told the others and continued the search. As the morning wore on, more neighbors heard the news and came to help. Before long the entire community was out looking for clues as to where Charlie might have been. Some of the ladies came along with their husbands to support Frankie and baby Nancy and to help take care of the children. Many of them brought food for the family and friends who came in to warm up and eat a bite before going back out on the search.

The group assembled again before leaving for their homes. They decided there was no reason to continue the search on the river. They would have to wait until the snow and ice melted and the river could be checked for his body. Most of them returned home cold, tired, and hungry from a hard day of climbing, walking, and searching. It had all been in vain. Many of them promised to go back and help the next day.

When Jacob returned with the results of the day's search, Frankie became completely hysterical. She screamed, "He must be dead. He must be dead, or you would've found him by now! What are we going to do? He must have drowned in the river. I may never see him again!"

Jacob explained to Frankie, "We will continue our search tomorrow, and we will not stop till we have found him. Frankie, did he get riled about something and leave in a tizzy? You don't think he'd just go off somewhere and leave you and the baby, do you?"

"No, he just said he was going to George Young's place to get some Christmas liquor. I asked him not to go 'cause he didn't need to be drinking so much, but he just took no heed and went on anyway."

"Has he been acting different? Have you noticed anything unusual lately? Has he been sick?" Jacob asked.

"Nothing out of the ordinary that I can recollect."

Again Frankie began to sob, and Jacob placed his arms around her. He assured her he would do everything in his power to find Charlie and bring him back.

The next day the search continued, this time with a smaller number of people. As before, the day started by checking on the little cabin again. When Charlie was not found there, the search widened to the tops of the mountains.

A searcher told Jacob, "Maybe he was hunting, and something happened to him out in the woods."

Jacob explained to them, "He would not have gone hunting without the trusty old rifle his grandfather gave him."

Al said, "I looked. It is still hanging above the door where he always keeps it, Dad."

They agreed to meet again at Jacob's house before ending the day. It was also agreed that if anyone found a clue or heard any word, they would return immediately to Jacob's house and sound his hunting horn.

Nancy tried hard to reassure Frankie that everything would be all right. On several occasions she tried to get Frankie to go over to the cabin and wait for Charlie there. She told Frankie she would go with her and help do anything she needed done at her house.

"I don't want to go over there without Charlie!" Frankie said and again burst into tears.

"I understand. I don't blame you. I thought it might just help you to get out of this house for a little while, that's all."

Jacob returned after another long fruitless day of searching. Many of the others had given up early and returned to their homes to do evening chores. He and Al joined the rest of the family on the porch to explain that the day had not been successful. Several more days passed with Jacob and Al still searching. Sometimes they searched alone.

When it had been a week since Charlie was last seen, there was some talk that he simply may have decided married life was not for him and hit the road. The people who knew him said Charlie would not have left his family like that. Almost everyone knew he really loved little Nancy and was very proud of his daughter.

The cold snap had gone, and the snow was beginning to melt. Jacob was pondering what his next step would be. Even though he was tired and weary he could not give up.

After talking with Nancy, he decided to encourage all the people searching not to give up and to look farther in all directions.

Frankie was refusing to eat anything. She looked miserable, as if she had lost the will to live. Her eyes were sunken, with dark circles around them, and flushed from the lack of sleep and continual weeping.

Nancy whispered to Jacob, "How long do you think she can go on like this?"

Jacob replied, "I don't know how any of us are going to be able to continue if we don't find Charlie soon. I have already put it in the Lord's hands, though."

Chapter Seven

The snow and ice had almost completely melted. Jacob and Al searched the river for miles, but there was still no sign of Charlie. Jacob checked the river directly below the place where the tracks had come out on the ice. He waded into the freezing, deep water searching for his son. Al got a fire going on the bank for him to warm and dry himself when he was done. Jacob remembered that the crack in the ice hadn't looked as though a person could have fallen through, but he wanted to make sure. He asked himself again why those tracks had gone out on the ice.

Several neighbors had returned to help in the search again. But when it proved fruitless again, they began to agree with Jacob that something strange and unexplainable had happened. It was a mystery to everyone who knew Charlie.

Soon word of Charlie's strange disappearance spread into the surrounding communities. Sheriff W. C. Butler had been notified of the matter and had made the long trip up from the county seat at Morganton to talk with the Silver family about it. He assured them he would do all he could to help locate their missing son.

The sheriff told an old settler friend about the missing man and asked him to help in finding any information leading to Charlie Silver's whereabouts. The old man's name was John Collis. He was a short, stocky man with a long, flowing white beard. He wore an old, floppy, worn-out coonskin cap and had rosy cheeks; bushy white eyebrows; small, tight, red lips; and just two or three teeth. He had a big hunting knife strapped to his wide, brown leather belt. John was known far and wide as an outstanding hunter and woodsman. He had been successful on other occasions in helping the sheriff solve incidents of missing persons.

The sheriff told all those who were searching, "I have asked a real sleuth to come assist us today. I want all of you to help him in any way you can. He will let you know when he needs something. I really appreciate him coming to give us a hand in the search for this young man."

After hearing that tracks had been found leading down toward the river, John decided to go there and look for any clues that might explain Charlie's mysterious absence. Finding nothing there he decided to go to the Silvers' place and find Jacob.

Jacob had become more and more distraught. He knew all the men who had scoured the mountainsides and valleys were skilled at climbing and knew every inch of the land in those parts. He also knew they wouldn't have left any possibility unexplored. So he really didn't know what to do next and welcomed any suggestions, including one from a neighbor who knew of a man who lived in Tennessee, a Negro slave who used a glass ball to find missing people.

Jacob told his family, "This seems a little far-fetched, but I have to do something. Shucks, what harm is there in seeing if there is any truth to this story?" He and Nancy decided if there was a remote possibility that it would help he would go locate this man.

Soon after he left, John Collis knocked on the door. Nancy answered and came out on the porch.

John removed his cap. "Howdy, ma'am. I am John Collis, and I am here helping the sheriff look for your son. Where might I find the man of the house?"

"I'm mighty pleased to meet you, sir. I do appreciate your taking the time to help us look for Charlie. My husband, Jacob, is going to see a man in Tennessee to help us look for our son. He may not be gone yet. He was going by Charlie's house one more time before he leaves. You just missed him."

Nancy continued talking to him about her missing son. He asked her as many questions as he could think of, including what Charlie looked like and what he had been wearing. He also asked her how long Charlie had been missing. Then he inquired where he might find Charlie's wife.

Nancy went to the door and called to Frankie, "There's a man named John Collis out here, and he wants to talk with you, Frankie! The sheriff has sent him."

Frankie had been standing in the living room out of sight, listening to the conversation. She came out on the front porch with Nancy.

"Mr. Collis, this is Frankie, Charlie's wife," said Mrs. Silver.

"Pleased to make your acquaintance, ma'am. I have a few questions for you. When did Charlie first leave?"

"He left just before dark saying he was going to George Young's to git some Christmas liquor," Frankie replied.

"What was he wearing?"

"He was wearing his brogan shoes and his heavy hunting coat."

"Why did he leave?"

"I told you—he said he wanted some Christmas liquor. He said he wanted some for medicine in case we got the croup. I begged him not to go, but he went on anyway."

He asked her many other questions and patiently waited each time for her answer.

"Now, my last question," said Mr. Collis. "Do you mind if I go over to your house and take a look around? You can go with me if you would like. I will need somebody to let me go in anyway."

"I would go with you, but every time I even think of that place without him, it only adds more to my grief. No, you go ahead and look around. I don't want to go back in that hollow again as long as I live."

Nancy told him, "The house is just around the hill, but I'll get John to go show you the way over there." She turned and called out, "Margaret, go tell John to put his coat on and come outside!"

Mr. Collis said, "That won't be necessary, ma'am. If it's just around the hill, I think I can find it by myself. Maybe Jacob will be there to let me in."

"Never mind, Margaret, just keep looking after the baby," Nancy called again to her daughter. "Mr. Collis, we appreciate your help and concern. If there's any way we can help you, please let us know."

He left the two women standing on the front porch. He then headed toward the cabin. Just as he rounded the curve at the top of the hill, he met the sheriff and several other men who were taking part in the search. They had already discussed their search plans with Jacob and Al. Jacob had told them about his plan to go to Tennessee. One of them had told Jacob politely he would only be wasting his time.

Jacob had sadly replied, "At this point I'll try or do anything if it will help me find my son."

John Collis found Jacob near Charlie's cabin getting ready to go to Tennessee. After introducing himself John asked Jacob. "Before you go will you come with me to take a gander inside and around the cabin?"

Jacob said, "I don't mind at all. I'll go to Tennessee after we finish."

"I would like to have someone in the family with me. The rest of you can come along if you would like."

The group headed their horses up the soggy road and along the branch toward the little log cabin. When they got off their horses, they tied them to some laurel bushes near the house.

Sheriff Butler called out, "Will some of you men take a look around in the yard? Check under the porch and out in the horse shed."

After checking the yard and the shed, the men started looking in the woods and the undergrowth of laurel and rhododendron just above the house.

After about an hour, Sheriff Butler called the searchers back and told them, "I don't think we are going to find anything here. Fellas, you have looked very hard and have done a great job. There's no sense in continuing our search. We might as well go. Who knows? He might have decided to leave her and never look back."

When Jacob heard this comment, it brought tears to his eyes. But he realized if the man had known Charlie, he wouldn't have said it.

John asked Jacob, "Will you open the door of the cabin to let me go in? Open them both—I'll need all the daylight I can get in there to see if there's anything that will help us."

Jacob opened both the back and front doors of the cabin. He pulled the peg and slid the board back to open the little window in order to let in all the available light. John slowly studied everything in the cabin. He felt and smelled almost everything. He had an odd frown on his face as he studied the situation.

The sheriff looked at John and asked, "What about it, John? Shall we go?"

The rest of the men had already gone outside and saddled up to leave. The sheriff, Jacob, and John were still inside, and just as they turned to join the others, John found an important clue as to Charlie's absence.

Meanwhile Frankie told Mrs. Silver as she pulled on her coat, "I am going to mosey over to see how the search is going. I'll be back before long."

This surprised Nancy at first, but she was glad Frankie was going to get out of the house for a little while.

Nancy told her, "I'll go with you."

"No, I'll go by myself. You take care of the children."

When Frankie crossed the hill and arrived just above the cabin, she saw the horses and men standing in the yard. She moved carefully because the crunch of the leaves and sticks might alert them to her presence.

As she went closer, a shout from inside the cabin suddenly drew the men's attention, and they made a rush for the back door. Her breath caught, and she drew closer until she could hear what was being said inside. The men were discussing what they had found, and she suddenly felt cold.

Frankie pushed her way through the group of men and ordered them out of her house. She screamed and swore at the top of her voice as they turned to face her. She could read the shock and accusations in their looks that told her what they suspected.

Chapter Eight

Frankie continued her wild threats and protest as the men resumed their search. As the shocking truth came together slowly like pieces of an ugly puzzle, Jacob felt his heart almost tearing from his chest. He looked at Frankie at first in disbelief, but as the men continued to find more evidence he was reluctantly convinced of Charlie's death. To make matters worse, everything seemed to point toward Frankie's guilt.

I must be having a horrible dream, Jacob thought as he sat on the edge of the bed with his face buried in his hands. *Surely this cannot be true.*

His thoughts were broken by Mr. Collis, who had just finished sifting through the ashes in the fireplace. There was a small pile of bone bits and teeth on the rock hearth. He commented on the unusual amount of ashes there.

Someone picked up the ax and called John's attention to the big gaps in its sharp, shiny edge.

Then John pointed out the recent hack marks on the rocks in the fireplace and the mantle, which was also covered with some kind of oil or grease as if someone had been rendering lard. The sheriff noticed how neatly the floor had been scrubbed and scoured until the tops of the logs looked like brand-new wood.

John decided to check the other sides of the floor logs. He asked the men to help him raise the puncheons. Several men used the ax and the shovel from the fireplace to help lift the logs. John did not seem surprised by what he found. The bottoms of the logs were covered with a dark substance that appeared to be dried blood. There was also a large patch on the ground below.

"He used to have a big bearskin rug there in front of the fireplace, and it's gone," Jacob whispered to the sheriff.

As the evidence continued to add up, it increasingly seemed to point an accusing finger at Frankie. She started toward the door but was stopped by the sheriff. He took her by the arm and said, "Young lady, you have some explaining to do. Did you kill your husband?"

Frankie had gone from anger to tears and was unable to speak. She only shook her head, indicating she had not killed her husband.

The sheriff asked, "How do you explain what we have found here in this house today, young lady?"

"I was rendering some lard. That's where the grease came from."

Jacob said softly without looking at her, "We have not killed a hog lately, Sheriff."

John got up from the fireplace, walked over to Frankie, and gently asked, "Did you kill your husband? You did, didn't you? These are human teeth, ma'am! How do you explain that?"

"I don't know. All I do know is I don't know anything about my husband's death."

"You said he was wearing his brogan shoes." He pointed toward the bed. "They are sitting over there by the bed. Explain that."

The sheriff went outside and asked Elisha Green to take a message to David Baker. He was an acting justice of the peace in the county. "Please return as quickly as possible with an answer from him."

The search now intensified inside and outside.

After a few minutes, one man called out to the others, "Come quick to the spring, and see what I've found out here!"

He had been poking around outside and made a horrifying discovery in a hole. When the others joined him, they saw the pieces of Charlie's body that had not burned.

The men started talking to one another.

"Frankie could not have done this dastardly deed by herself. It just seems impossible for such a pretty little young woman to commit such a crime alone."

Another said, "Could this little girl have the guts or the strength to do this without someone helping her?"

As they openly considered the possibility, one person said, "Maybe her father or brother helped her with this! I saw Barbara and Blackston Stuart heading home on December twenty-second. They could have helped her."

Another responded, "Why don't you go in and tell the sheriff what we have been talking about? Tell him you saw the Stuarts heading home on the day Charlie went missing."

The man returned to the cabin and told the sheriff what they had found outside and the possibility that Frankie's mother and brother had helped her. Jacob's nightmare continued to worsen. The sheriff began to question Frankie once again.

"Were any of your family here at this house any time around December twenty-second?"

Frankie mumbled, "Yes, they were here. Mother and Blackston came over to visit us before Christmas and brought some gifts she had made for me and the baby."

"Did they have anything to do with your husband's death?" the sheriff asked with a stern voice.

"I don't know anything about my husband's death. Sir, I have told you before. I wish you all would leave me alone. Can't you see we can't find my husband? Why do you folks want to torture me?"

Al, who had been helping in the search, suddenly left in tears to tell his mother and the rest of the family what had been found. When he told Nancy, she gasped.

In a stern, defensive tone she said, "That is absolutely not true, Al. Frankie loves Charlie and did not do such a horrible thing!"

She studied Al's tearful face and slowly broke down weeping and wailing. Al tried to comfort her, fighting his own sobs and tears. She threw her arms up and screamed, "No, no. Why, God? Not again! What have we done to pay such an awful price? Charlie is such a dear boy. This will be the end of my poor Jacob. What are we going to do? Why, Lord, why?"

The rest of the children had gathered around and were crying loudly as they held on to their mother. They were all gradually realizing that something horrible must have happened to their big brother.

"I have to go back to be with Dad," Al told Nancy. "I don't want him there without one of us. There is still a large number of people over there checking for other evidence."

Al made his way back to the little cabin and found his dad sitting outside on the steps, his trembling hands covering his face as he sobbed. He was barely able to catch his breath. When he saw Al, he managed to get up and throw his arms around his son's neck, and they both wept bitterly. Some of the men tried to comfort them, but nothing much could help in that heart-breaking moment.

Later the same afternoon, as the sun was sinking behind the mountains, Elisha Green returned to the cabin on a horse that was quite lathered from its fast and furious ride. Elisha took an envelope from his saddlebag and handed it to Sheriff Butler, who opened it as the men gathered around. He took out the wrinkled paper and began to read as Frankie, Jacob, Al, and the whole group listened intently.

> This day came Elisha Green before me, D. D. Baker, an acting justice of said county, and made oath in due form of law that Frankie Silver and Barbara Stuart—it is believed they did murder Charles Silver contrary to law and against the dignity of the state. Sworn to and subscribed by me this ninth day of January 1832.

> At the bottom of this note Elisha Green had signed his name.

Elisha Green

There are therefore to command some lawful offi-
cer to take the bodies of the above-named Frankie
Silver and Barbara Stuart and Blackston Stuart
and them safely keep so you have them before me
or some other justice of said county to answer the
above charge and to be further dealt with according
as the law directs. Given under my hand and seal,
this the ninth day of January 1832.

D. D. Baker, J. P.

Walking over to Frankie, who was now standing on the steps near
the doorway of the house, the sheriff placed handcuffs on her and led
her into the yard.

"Please, sir, you can't do this to me. I have a little child. I can't go
to jail. I have a little baby!"

The sheriff pretended not to hear her. He told the constable he
would take the warrant to the Stuarts and make the arrests of Mrs.
Stewart and Blackston. Turning to the other men present, he asked
for some to accompany him in this duty.

"We will need to hurry. Wait here a while," he said to the constable, "and then I want you and the other men to join me with Frankie
back at the crossroads near the Silvers' place."

Before he left to go after the Stuarts, the sheriff went to Jacob and
told him in a sympathetic voice, "Mr. Silver, I am so sorry about what
has happened here and what we have found today. Give the rest of your
family my sincere condolences. Oh, do you mind if we use Charlie's
horse to take Frankie into Morganton? I would certainly appreciate it. I will send him back to you as soon as we have her locked up."

Jacob was unable to respond, so Al nodded and whispered between
his sobs, "It's all right. Go ahead and take him."

The sheriff thanked them and rode off to make the arrests of Barbara and Blackston Stuart.

The rest of the men got Dan from the shed and put Frankie on him. Both Jacob and Al refused to look at her. This was more than a horrible nightmare. How could such a thing be happening? Their hearts had been gradually and deceitfully ripped out of them. It was more than either man could handle or begin to understand.

The constable told them he planned to take the prisoners on to Morganton to be kept locked up until a trial could be held. He asked Al if they could have some food to take with them. Both Al and Jacob nodded and the men went back to the house with sacks from their saddlebags to gather up a little food for the trip.

Some of the party had mounted their horses and were talking loudly so Frankie could hear them. A man shouted an accusing remark at her. Frankie did not respond, but the constable looked at him and told him to save that for later.

The group started making their way down the road by the branch. The melting snow and the large number of horses coming and going had almost made the little road impassable. Frankie was on Dan, led by the constable. She kept her head bowed with her hair covering most of her face.

She thought of the good times she'd had in the little cabin and cove she was leaving behind. *Why is all this happening?* She wondered. *I just don't understand.* She thought of the happy trips she and Charlie had made up and down this little trail. It hurt to think they were all over now.

Then her thoughts went to her child, and tears again streamed from her bloodshot eyes. She had to see little Nancy again before she went to jail. She knew it would mean facing Charlie's mother and the rest of the family, but she was willing to pay that unbearable price.

She slowly raised her head and asked without looking at the constable, "Please, sir, can I go see my baby before we leave?"

The constable didn't say a word but kept on riding.

When they reached the crossroads, they stopped and dismounted to wait for the sheriff. Frankie remained on old Dan. There was once again mumblings and looks of hate from the group as they walked around waiting for the sheriff to return.

Jacob and Al left the group and rode on home to be with the rest of the family.

One man with a scowling face walked over to Frankie and shouted at her, "We should do the same thing to you that you did to Charlie! I can't believe you could do such a thing. I'll bet you put on his boots and walked down to the river in the snow and then walked backward in the same tracks! You were trying to make it look like he fell through the ice. I believe you even threw a rock to break it! That's all I can figure. You sure are a smart little hussy."

The Constable responded loudly, "Mister, I am telling you all now, you are not to harass the prisoner! Just mind your own business. To answer your question, Mrs. Silver, that decision about seeing your baby will be entirely up to the Sheriff Butler when he gets here."

Constable Baker was very concerned about the long journey back to Morganton. It was getting late. Getting all three prisoners locked up in jail would not be an easy task, and they had a long ride ahead of them. He could feel the men's tension. Many had spent days looking for Charlie and were infuriated Frankie had known where he was all that time. He was not worried about the sheriff because he was accustomed to the mountain people and knew what to expect from them much better than the constable did.

The sheriff arrived before long and was greeted by the constable and some of the other men. He had Barbara and Blackston cuffed and on separate horses led by several of the men who had gone with him. Frankie looked at her mother and brother while they were nearing the group but then dropped her head as if she didn't want to see them.

Barbara shouted, "We are all innocent! We did not have anything to do with the disappearance of Charlie Silver. Y'all will have to prove what you are accusing us of. My husband will make you all pay for this."

"That's enough, Mrs. Stuart. You have made your plea over and over. You will get your chance to explain everything to a jury," the sheriff answered calmly and carefully.

The large group mounted and headed toward the town of Morganton. They moved in complete silence until they reached the Silvers' place.

Frankie couldn't stand it any longer, so she cried to the sheriff with a pleading voice, "Please, sir. Oh please, let me see my child before we leave."

"You should have thought about her before now, miss! I'll let you go by and see her, but only for a few minutes. I will go in with you as I can't let you out of my sight for one second. We have to get to Morganton as soon as we can. We need to make it to the foot of these mountains by nightfall, which means we will have to ride hard."

Someone in the crowd spoke up. "They always say you can't trust a woman. It sure is true in this case."

Another spoke up. "Hell has no fury like that of a woman."

The sheriff interrupted the exchange. "It is best for you fellas to keep your comments to yourselves. I understand exactly how you feel, but you just need to leave her alone!"

When they came to the road leading down toward the Silver family's log home Frankie and the sheriff left the others standing in the road. Frankie hoped she would not have to face Nancy, but as they went near the house, Mrs. Silver came out on the porch holding the baby. The sheriff dismounted and helped Frankie down from the horse and up to the porch. Mrs. Silver turned as if she were going back into the house but then paused, turned, and took a few steps toward Frankie. With tears streaming from her eyes, she held the baby out to her.

Frankie could not hold the baby because of the handcuffs, but she leaned up against her and gave her a long and desperate kiss. Then she let out a mournful wail. "Oh God, what is happening?" The baby started crying when the sheriff pulled Frankie away and led her back to the horse. He helped her mount. She kept looking back and screaming as they started toward the waiting posse.

Jacob and Al and the rest of the family came out on the porch as they were leaving. The sheriff saw them and called back to Jacob, "Mr. Silver, please round up as many witnesses as you can find and get them to the courthouse as soon as possible."

Jacob called back, "I'll do the best I can, Sheriff. I'm much obliged to ye for your help in solving this. Be careful as you go back down the mountain. I will always be beholden to ye. Al and I will round up some witnesses."

They were all sobbing as the group left them and headed back to Morganton. Only a few days earlier, the Silver family had had such love and admiration in their hearts for Frankie.

Lucinda asked, "Mama, why do they think Frankie hurt Charlie?"

None of them were able to grasp the gravity of what had happened. Would their Christian faith keep them from hating the one who, like Charlie, had held such a special place in all their hearts?

Jacob put his arms around Nancy and commented, "It seems to me that each time we are visited by death in our family, it brings with it a sting that is even more unbearable than before. I think it is bad enough to lose someone because of natural causes, but this is so hard to accept. That was my Charlie."

Faces that had once been filled with bright smiles were now clouded by grief and sorrow. They hurt for the family member who had meant so much to them, but there had also been a great love there for Frankie.

The sheriff and constable kept a good lookout for some of the prisoners' relatives that might ambush the group as they rode along.

Isaiah Stuart had made threats and promises to the sheriff when he'd arrested Barbara and Blackston. He would have gone for his rifle, but the sheriff had surprised him before he had time.

"I will come after the three of them with my brother," Isaiah had told the sheriff. "I will have them with us when we get back home! I have no intention of leaving this in the hands of the dirty law."

Sheriff Butler knew that Isaiah could make good on those threats. He was not taking any chances. He told the others to be on the look-out for any strange noises or anyone following them as they made their journey down the long dirt road.

When they reached the foot of the mountains, it was getting dark. They stopped to make camp for the night. They rested the horses and let them drink. When the prisoners had dismounted, Frankie asked to relieve herself.

The sheriff told Frankie, "You can't leave my sight. You can go behind those bushes. I will have this pistol aimed at you in case you try to run." He then let Barbara take her turn. For Blackston he instructed Constable Baker, "Follow him into the woods and let him do his business. Keep a pistol aimed at him at all times. If he tries to run, well, in that case it won't be wrong to shoot a prisoner in the back."

As he was letting Blackston relieve himself, Constable Baker heard a stick break in the woods near where they were. He yelled for the sheriff almost in a panic. Several men came running and heard the sound of hoof beats leaving the place where he said he'd heard the sound. The men rode in the direction of the sound and found nothing. They soon went back to join the others.

One of them said, "I'll bet that was Isaiah. He is an ornery old cuss. He knows better than to go up against the best guns in Burke County. That includes you, Sheriff Butler."

They got some fresh water from a nearby stream and got a camp-fire going. They took turns guarding their three prisoners as they ate some of the cold, stale bread and side meat the Silvers had given them before their long trek to Morganton.

After a long and restless night, the group rose at dawn, doused the fire, and mounted up for the remainder of their trip. When they reached the outskirts of town, the residents of Morganton came out of their houses to meet them as news had already spread quickly. It had stunned the entire state. People wanted to see what a woman who could commit such a heinous crime looked like.

It was late afternoon as the slow-moving group rode with their prisoners through the streets. Frankie, her mother, and her brother all kept their heads down in order to avoid the shouts and sneers from the angry onlookers.

At one point Blackston raised his head long enough to shout back, "I don't know any more about his death than you do!"

Someone yelled back, "That may well be true, but that little blonde sister of yours knows something."

Standing in the middle of this angry mob were Ellie Maude Murphy and Eliza G. Burgner.

"Well, Ellie Maude," said Eliza, "I am surprised to see you here. We missed you at church last night. I thought you might be taken down with something. You do look a mite peaked."

"No, Eliza, I was there. I came in late and had to sit in the back instead of my usual place in the front. I was late because I ran into Bessie on the street. You know Bessie—she can talk the ears off of an old mule. She started telling me about this awful murder over in the Toe River section. Shucks, I came to see that gal what killed her husband in cold blood. When I heard they were bringing her in, I dropped everything to skedaddle down here to see her. Looks like I'm not the only one by the size of this crowd."

"Wait till I tell Bessie you said she could talk the ears off of an old mule. Where did she get all this gossip?"

"I don't know, but she said the husband was tired from chopping wood all day and stacking it in the corner of the house before the big snow came. So he fell asleep in front of the warm fire on his bearskin rug while holding their child. The wife took their sleeping baby from his loving arms, and, while he slept, she killed him."

"Well, this may not be true, but someone told me he was mean to her. They said he beat her. A friend of mine who talked to Frankie's mother said that she told her Charlie was seeing another woman and was fixing to run off with her. This was told to me by a reliable source from across the mountain. What do you think? I think she was just trying to defend herself."

"Naw hesh your mouth. I don't believe one word of it. He is from a fine, outstanding family, and 'sides, that was not reason enough to make her do such an awful thing?"

"Well, I will say there certainly comes a point when a person has to defend himself. I don't know for sure, but I really do believe he provoked her. It could just be the idea that if I can't have him no one else will."

Some of the crowd followed the procession as it came to the big courthouse in the center of town. It was now dusk, as the sun had slipped behind table rock. The sheriff told the constable and posse to help bring the prisoners inside as he followed with a watchful eye and his revolver at the ready.

Once they were within, the sheriff put the two women in one cell and Blackston in another. He told the constable to go down to the boarding house on the corner and tell Doshie Burgin to fetch some food to the courthouse—enough to feed three prisoners and the posse.

As the evening wore on, the crowd outside the courthouse seemed to grow bigger by the minute. The sheriff did not fancy having a lynch mob on his hands. As this seemed to be a growing possibility, he decided to let the posse return home as soon as they were fed because he suspected they were helping to agitate the crowd.

He went outside on the steps and called them inside. "I want you all to go inside and wait in the courtroom until the constable gets back with some food for your supper. After you eat I want you to head back home. I appreciate all your help, and I know you all are very tired. I know I am."

The constable finally arrived with food from the boarding house. He fed the group and sent them back across the mountain.

When they had left, the sheriff told Constable Baker, "After you finish eating, I want you to go see a friend of mine. His name is Wardell Morrison. Tell him to round up some of our local men to help. I'll deputize them to guard the courthouse and jail till things cool down some. Can you also go by the office of your cousin, the justice of the peace, and tell him the three suspects are safely tucked away in jail."

Constable Baker did as asked. He poked his head into his cousin's office and said, "You're working late, aren't you? Sheriff Butler asked me to tell you that the three murder suspects are safely locked in jail."

The justice of the peace responded, "I'm glad to see you made it! Judging from the talk around town, you folks could have had your hands full bringing them in. There are a lot of people riled up over this mess."

Late the next day, Jacob arrived with five witnesses he had rounded up from the Toe River Valley. He sent the small group to the office of the justice of the peace. While there the justice of the peace made the following entry in his big log book:

"The defendants committed to jail on the oath of Thomas Howeland, William Hutchins, Nancy Wilson, Elander Silver, Margaret Silver, and upon the word of the jury. This 10th day of January 1832. D. D. Baker, J.P."

The next day, back across the mountain, an unusual funeral for Charlie was held at the Kona Baptist Church. There was no casket. Several different graves had already been dug and filled as parts of Charlie's grisly remains had been discovered. There were three separate stones placed at these sites. The burial, such as it was, had already been done.

People brought food to the Silvers' home and stayed with them far into the night. They were accustomed to sitting up with the dead, but this was unusual because there was no body. The whole community mourned the loss of Charlie.

The next day the family made its way up the hill to the little church, which was already filled to overflowing. The people stood as the family filed in and sat in the front.

The preacher started with scripture. "Oh death, where is thy sting? Oh grave, where is thy victory?" He comforted them by telling them, "You all grieve now, but one glorious day you will see him again in heaven. Let not your hearts be troubled. Ye believe in God. Believe also in me. In my father's house are many mansions. If it were not so, I would have told you. I go to prepare a place for you, and if I go, I shall come again to receive you unto myself that where I am there you may be also.

"Family, the greatest comfort I can give you in this trying hour is that I can remember when Charlie got religion right here in this here altar. I don't know his heart, but I believe he truly got religion. I'm sure many of you recollect when he was baptized. Thank God for that blessed memory."

The family and friends were sobbing and wiping their eyes.

The preacher told them, "Please, don't weep as those who have no hope. You will see him again!"

There was a big, loud chorus of "amen."

There were several songs sung, including "Amazing Grace," and several people testified about what a good young man Charlie had been. The preacher asked the men of the church to gather at the altar as he dismissed them in prayer.

Afterward many neighbors and friends gathered around the family to offer their condolences. When the family exited the church, they looked down at Charlie's little now-empty cabin. It now stood as an ugly reminder of the whole tragic event.

They went back down the hill, just as they had many times before, still grieving over their beloved son. They knew that only time would help heal their broken hearts.

Chapter Nine

Frankie and Blackston, along with their mother, were all safe in jail. And judging from the public opinion, they would be there to stay. The people of the county were all excited and curious about the unusual case. The justice of the peace put all the witnesses under bond to ensure their appearances at the trial. The local paper carried the story, and everyone in the surrounding areas was talking about the horrible and grisly murder up on the Toe River.

The prisoners knew that Isaiah Stuart would not give up easily. They knew at this very moment he was somewhere working toward their freedom. He had been to talk with two of the best lawyers in the area, Joseph McDowell and Isaac T. Avery, to see if they would defend his family in court.

He'd told them, "I will get the money, even if I have to sell everything I own, if you will just take the case." McDowell refused because he was already involved in a big land dispute. Avery also refused and it may have been due to the publicity that had been generated by the case. Another lawyer, Theodore W. Wilson, finally accepted the challenge but explained to Isaiah, "I will take it with much reluctance due to the extreme amount of publicity and prejudice that surrounds your case. I will need to question Frankie, Blackston, and Barbara before I can tell you how I will handle the lawsuit."

Isaiah and Wilson arrived in Morganton several days later on the morning of January 13. The town had already started to bustle. There were a few horses tied up in front of the courthouse, and some of the storekeepers were busy opening their businesses and sweeping the sidewalks. Isaiah and Wilson made their way straight through town to the courthouse and to the office of the justice of the peace.

Isaiah took the advice of his lawyer and told two of the acting justices that the defendants were being held unjustly. He told them the defendants were not guilty and had not been given a chance to prove their innocence.

Lawyer Wilson also told the justices it was unlawful to hold the prisoners without giving them the chance to face their accusers.

Justice Hughes countered with, "They will get their chance when they are tried in a court of law. Which will be as soon as possible."

The two sitting justices made the following entry into the court record books:

> North Carolina—Burke County. Whereas Isaiah Stuart has complained to us, John C. Burginor and Thomas Hughes, two of the sitting justices of the peace and for the County of Burke aforesaid, that Barbara Stuart, Frankie Silver, and Blackston Stuart have been suspected of having committed a murder on the body of one Charles Silver, and whereas it has been made to appear on both of the said Isaiah Stuart that the said defendants have been committed to the common jail of the county aforesaid without legal forms of trial and without the parties having it in their power of confronting their accusers before any legal tribunal: There are, therefore, to command you, Sheriff of Burke County or any other lawful officer of said County, to arrest the bodies of Barbara Stuart, Frankie Silver, and Blackston Stuart, and them safely keep so that you have them before us at Morganton within the time prescribed by law, then and there to answer the charge and to be further dealt with as the law directs. Here in fail, not at your peril.

Given from under our hands and seal, this 13th
day of January, A. D. 1832.

Thos. Hughes, J. P.
J. C. Burginor, J. P.

The habeas corpus proceeding was only four days later, on
January 17. Barbara and Blackston had talked with the justice of
the peace and seemed to have a good argument.

The following record written by two of the justices states:

Defendants Barbara Stuart and Blackston Stuart plead not guilty
on the 17th day of January, 1832 warrant returned before us, John
C. Burginor and Aaron Brittain, Esquires. The defendants being
brought before us to –wit: Barbara Stuart and Blackston Stuart, and
on examination of the evidence, we are of the opinion that the defendants should be discharged, there appearing no evidence on behalf of
the State against them.

Barbara and Blackston were placed under heavy bond of one hundred pounds and bound over to appear at the March 1832, term of
the Superior Court in Burke County. Isaiah went on the bond for
security.

Frankie did not appear before the justices.

The superior court didn't convene until March 17, 1832. Isaiah
and his lawyer worked hard on the case during the weeks that followed. Meanwhile Frankie spent many restless nights in that cramped,
dingy jail cell. She hated that horrible cold and smelly place. Longing
to have her freedom, she stood looking out the tiny barred window.
She wanted desperately to see her baby. Time moved so slowly for
her now. Days seemed like weeks, and weeks dragged into long and
restless months. All she could do was sit and think. She thought of

Charlie and the love they once had for each other. The first time he walked her home. Their wedding and wedding night. She tried to reason what had brought about the changes in Charlie. Then her thoughts turned again to her little child. The sheriff often found her sitting on her bed crying.

His Honor Judge John R. Donnell, Esquire, was in town along with many of the witnesses and hordes of observers. The courthouse was rumbling with excitement until the bailiff walked in with Frankie, Barbara and Blackston. A complete hush came over the crowd when she entered the courtroom. Frankie took her place at the front with her lawyer, Mr. Wilson. Her head was bowed and she didn't look into the audience.

Judge Donnell rapped his gavel several times and called the court to order. After a Grand Jury of eighteen men were selected Judge Donnell then said, "I am going to ask the prosecutor William Alexander from Charlotte, North Carolina to read the bill of indictment." He stood and read the following:

> State of North Carolina, Burke County Superior Court of Law, spring term 1832.
>
> The jurors for the state, upon their oath, present that Frances Silver, Blackston Stuart, and Barbara Stuart, all of said county, not having the fear of God before their eyes but being moved and seduced by the instigation of the devil, on the twenty-second day of December in the year of our Lord one thousand and eight hundred and thirty-one, with force and arms in the County of Burke aforesaid, in and upon one Charles Silver in the peace of God and of the state, then and there being feloniously, willfully, and of malice aforethought did make an assault; and that the said Frances Silver, with a certain ax

of the value of six pence, which the said Frances Silver in both the hands of her, the said Frances, then and there had and held to, against and upon the said Charles Silver, then and there feloniously, willfully, and of her malice, aforethought did cast and throw; and that the said Frances Silver with the ax aforesaid so cast and thrown, as aforesaid, the said Charles Silver in and upon the head of him, the said Charles Silver, then and there feloniously, willfully, and of her malice and aforethought with the ax aforesaid, so as aforesaid by the said Frances Silver cast and thrown in and upon the head of him, the said Charles Silver, one mortal wound of the length of three inches and of the depth of one inch; of which said mortal wound he, the said Charles Silver, then and there instantly died; and that the said Blackston Stuart and Barbara Stuart at the time of committing the felony and murder aforesaid by the said Frances Silver in manner and form aforesaid, feloniously, willfully, and of their malice aforethought were present, aiding, helping, abetting, assisting, comforting, and maintaining the said Frances Silver in the felony and murder aforesaid in manner and form aforesaid to do, commit, and perpetrate, and so the jurors aforesaid, upon their oath aforesaid, do say that the said Frances Silver, Blackston Stuart, and Barbara Stuart, him, the said Charles Silver, in manner and form aforesaid feloniously, willfully, and of their malice aforethought did kill and murder against the peace and dignity of the state.

Wm. Alexander, Solicitor

The solicitor then took his seat with a low sigh of completion. After he had finished reading the long bill of indictment.

The trio was brought before the bar to enter their plea. They all three entered a plea of "Not Guilty."

The trial for Barbara and Blackston finally got underway. Then the witnesses were called to testify. They placed their right hands on the Bible and swore, "To tell the truth, the whole truth and nothing but the truth so help me God."

After long hours of testimony and argument, the judge instructed the jury to take the testimony of the witnesses that had been called to reach a decision concerning the guilt or innocence of Barbara and Blackston Stuart. They retired to the jury room and before long came back with the verdict of "not guilty" for Barbara and Blackston. The jury foreman remarked, "There was not sufficient evidence to connect these two directly to this murder, Your Honor."

The judge ordered Frankie to remain in the hands of the law. Due to the intense feeling that overshadowed the case, the judge ordered the sheriff to summon one hundred and fifty jurors to appear on the following Thursday. It was an unusual move and showed that the judge wanted to have a truly impartial jury. This move only prolonged the much-dreaded time that Frankie had been spending in that lonely jail cell.

Chapter Ten

On Thursday morning, March 29, 1832, a week following the release of her mother and brother, Frankie was again brought before the bar. She spent days sitting in the courtroom while jurors were questioned before being permitted to serve. Each night she returned to her cell and her agonizing thoughts and turmoil. The judge called the court to order and announced that the trial would begin with the selection of jurors. This was a long and arduous process with most of the prospective jurors being sent home. Finally the jury of twelve was seated. The judge looked at the lawyers and asked if they were ready for the trial to begin. He banged his gavel several times, calling the court back into order. An instant hush came over the crowded courtroom. It was packed with spectators in every corner and in the balcony. Many were not able to come inside but stood outside hoping to hear the proceedings from the open windows.

Finally twelve were sworn in out of the one hundred and fifty potential jurors:

Henry Pain, Cyrus P. Connelly, Joseph Tippts, Robert McElrath, John Hall, Lafayette Collins, David Beedle, William L. Baird, Robert Garrison, Oscar Willis, Richard Bean, and David Hennessee.

The big day of the trial had finally arrived. Frankie welcomed it. She wanted to get out of the cell that had been her horrible world for the past two miserable months.

Frankie's father and her lawyer, Theodore W. Wilson, were sitting at the front. Barbara and Blackston were sitting directly behind them. Barbara continuously wiped tears from her eyes. A crowd packed the courtroom again. An even bigger crowd had gathered outside.

His Honor Judge John R. Donnell, Esquire, was back in town along with many of the witnesses and hordes of observers. The courthouse was rumbling with excitement until the bailiff walked in with Frankie. A complete hush came over the crowd when she entered the courtroom. Frankie took her place at the front with her lawyer, Mr. Wilson. Her head was bowed and she didn't look into the audience.

Judge Donnell rapped his gavel several times and called the court to order. He then said, "I am going to ask the prosecutor William Alexander to read the bill of indictment." He stood and read the same bill of indictment that he read for the original hearing. He then announced this is a true bill of indictment as to Francis Silver but not a true bill as to the others.

The judge asked, "Mrs. Silver, how do you plead?"

"Not guilty, your honor" came Frankie's quiet plea.

Judge Donnell stated, "I am going to ask the lawyers for both sides to make their opening arguments. We will begin with William Alexander the prosecutor.

Lawyer Alexander stood again and looked briefly at a paper on his table, then approached the jury.

"Gentlemen of the jury I stand before you representing a young man whose life was taken from him around the twenty-second of December, 1831. His earthly life was cut short by people he trusted and loved. I will show you evidence that this terrible crime was committed by members of his own family.

Charles Silver was a loving and caring family man. He was devoted to his wife and daughter, Nancy. Besides the evidence of his murder I will also show a motive that will shed some light on this horrible and dastardly murder.

Charlie grew up in Kona. There he grew into a young and talented man who was respected and loved by the members of his community. He was the oldest son of Reverend Jacob Silver. Charles had an easy going personality and was a good law-abiding citizen. He was a member of Kona Baptist Church and attended regularly there."

He turns and points at Mr. and Mrs. Silver. "I stand before you asking you to listen to the case and put yourself in the place of Reverend and Mrs. Silver who have lost a dear and loving son. They nurtured and loved this son from a baby as they watched him grow into a young man. They instilled respect and character in all their children.

Charlie cannot be here today to speak for himself. Gentlemen of the jury, so I ask you to put yourself in his place and represent him today.

One of the Ten Commandments in the Holy Bible says, "Thou shalt not kill." There should be consequences for taking another's life and it will be your job to bring the murder or murderers to justice in this court of law.

I know there is a passel of publicity and talk concerning this case. I also know feelings are running high. However; I ask you to look only at the facts and what actually happened in this case.

The defendant's lawyer, Mr. Wilson will try to paint you a different picture of Charles Silver. He will have you believe Charlie was not a good and honorable man. That is his job! Charles Silver had his faults. I ask each of you to look at yourselves and ask if you are perfect. There was only one perfect human being who walked this earth and that was Jesus Christ.

I am asking you to weigh the facts and fulfill your responsibility to the State of North Carolina. Thank you. That's all Your Honor."

The judge looked at lawyer Wilson and said, "You may proceed with your opening statement Mr. Wilson."

Mr. Wilson had been studying the jury and watching their expressions while the prosecutor presented his opening statement. He had also been making numerous notes on his pad on the table. He stood slowly and buttoned his big baggy coat and walked over to the jury box.

"Gentlemen of the jury, I appreciate you serving on this case. It is not an easy task and one not to be taken lightly."

He turns and looks at the crowd.

"I also realize that there is tremendous speculation, rumors, gossip, and falsehoods surrounding this case. I simply ask that you follow your heart and the facts and then reach your verdict in this case.

I am representing a young lady, Francis Stuart Silver who was a loyal and dedicated wife to her husband Charles. She is a loving and dedicated mother to her daughter Nancy. There is not one blemish on the character of my client. She too is a good law-abiding citizen of Burke County.

Gentlemen, keep in mind it is the duty of the prosecutor to prove without a shadow of a doubt the guilt in this case. That is his job! I simply ask you to look at this young mother and ask if she could have committed such a crime against someone she loved."

Turning and pointing to Frankie, "Francis Silver was a good homemaker who was well respected in her community. She also attended church with her husband and baby. She had many talents and was a virtuous woman.

The loss of her husband has devastated her. Please keep in mind only she is left to look after her little child. Don't let these trumped up charges take her away from what family she has left.

Again I am asking you to look only at truth and facts as you consider this case. Thank you. That's all Your Honor."

Looking at the prosecutor the judge said, "Mr. Alexander, you may call your first witness."

Alexander stood and said, "Your Honor I am going to call Margaret Silver to the stand."

The deputy asked her to place her hand on the Bible and asked her, "Do you swear to tell the whole truth and nothing but the truth so help you God."

"I do." Came Margaret's reply.

Alexander approached the witness box after she was seated and asked, State your name for the record please.

"Margaret Silver."

"How do you know Charles Silver?"

"He is my oldest brother."

"What kind of brother was Charles?"

"What do you mean?"

"How did he treat you?"

"He was always kind and looked after me and my other brothers and sisters. He was not a selfish brother.' She began to sob. "It was a lot of fun to be around him."

"Was he ever mean to you?"

"No."

"Sometimes we would argue like most brothers and sisters, but he was never mean."

"How did you get along with the defendant Francis Silver?"

"Just fine I liked her very much."

"How did she treat Charles?"

"She was always good to him but she was a very jealous person. I noticed when any young woman talked to him she tried to stop the conversation and gave them a mean look. She was very possessive of him."

Lawyer Alexander turned to the judge and stated, "No further questions your honor."

"Mr. Wilson."

Mr. Wilson stood and said, "I have no question of this witness, Your Honor.

Mr. Alexander, you may call your next witness.

"I am calling Nancy Wilson to the stand, Your Honor."

After she was sworn in and seated he asked, "Please state your name."

"Nancy Wilson, sir"

"Did you know Charles Silver?"

"I have known him all my life. My brother's wife Lee Anna Wilson delivered Charles and Frankie's baby daughter. I remember Lee Anna saying she had never seen such love and devotion from a husband. She has delivered bunches of babies. She is a good midwife.

Lawyer Wilson jumped to his feet and called, "Objection, Your Honor that is hearsay."

The judge replied, "Sustained."

"I know his family also they are one of the finest families in the area. I have never heard anything but good about Charles or any of their children."

"Did you know Francis Silver his wife?"

"Not very well or as long, but she seemed to be a nice person. She and Charlie kept to themselves after they were married so I was not around her a lot. I do know Charles family was all very fond of her. If you ask me she…"

Mr. Alexander raised his hand to stop her and said, "No further question."

"Mr. Wilson"

He replied, "I have no question for the witness Your Honor."

"Mr. Alexander, your next witness."

Mr. Alexander stood and called Mr. Thomas Howeland to the stand where he was sworn in.

"State your name for the record please."

"Thomas Howeland."

"Mr. Howeland did you know Charles Silver from over in Kona.

"Yes."

"Tell us how you knew him."

"I live in the same area across the mountain where Charles lived."

"How long have you know him?"

"I have known him all his life. I remember when he was born. I am a neighbor and friend of Jacob and Nancy Silver."

"What kind of young man was Charles?"

"He was a fine fellow. I saw him as a hard worker and a talented member of our community."

"What do you know about Charles Silver's death?"

"Well, I was part of the search party that searched for days and weeks for Charlie when he went missing. I was still helping look when the Sheriff came with Mr. Collis to help find Charlie. The sheriff told us to look outside while he and Mr. Collis looked inside the house. Some of us men were outside looking and I found part of Charlie's body in a hollow stump covered with ashes. The remains appeared to be burned."

"Did you tell the sheriff?"

"Yes, we called him along with the others out there to the spring and showed him what I had found."

"What happened next?"

"The sheriff examined and made notes about what remained of the head and torso. He then informed me that Mr. Collis had already determined that Charlie had been killed in the house."

"What did you do next?'

"I asked the sheriff if I could remove the remains and get some of the men to help me give them a proper burial."

"No further questions, Your Honor."

The judge asked, "Do you want to question this witness Mr. Wilson?"

"Yes"

"Mr. Howeland, how did you know the remains were Charles Silver? Did you know for sure it was Charles Silver? Answer yes or no!

"Well, we had been looking..."

"Mr. Howeland, yes or no!"

"No, but he was the one missing and it was his place."

"You still don't know without a doubt, do you Mr. Howeland?"

"No"

"Do you know without a doubt who placed these remains there?'

"No."

Turning sharply he said, "You may step down." He walked over and threw his papers on the table and with a scowling look flopped into his seat.

"Mr. Alexander your next witness."

"Your Honor, I would like to call Mr. John Collis."

Mr. Collis waddled to the front. He was still dirty and untidy and carrying his coonskin cap in his hand. The deputy swore him in. Then he was seated in the witness box. He stroked his long white beard nervously as he looked at the huge crowd. His bald head was almost as white as the ring of hair that surrounded it.

Mr. Alexander said, "State your name for the record please."

"I am John Collis."

"How do you know the deceased Charles Silver?"

"Well, I'd never heard of him till I went to help the sheriff look fer him. I never had the pleasure of knowing him. As I said, the sheriff asked me if I would go with him to Kona and help him look fer this missing young man. I have helped him a lots of times before. He told me he had been missing for some time and was still missing. I agreed to go with him and see jes what I could find out."

"What did you find?"

"Well, while I wuz there I went to the river and looked around 'cause someone said he might have drowned. Then I went to the Jacob Silver place and talked with his wife. I asked Charles Silver's wife Francis a bunch of questions like, why he left and what he was wearing. She said he was wearing his old coat and his brogan shoes. Then I asked if I could go to their house and take a gander around and inside. While I talked with her I made up my mind that her behavior was unbecoming fer a woman hoping her husband would be coming home soon. I met Jacob Silver and his son Al near the house and they let me in. The first thing that got my attention was Charlie's shoes sitting near the bed. Then I noticed the large amount of ashes in the fireplace and grease all around the opening and on the mantle. I started sifting through the ashes and found bits of bone and teeth. I soon realized they were human teeth. I asked two fellows to help me lift the floor logs and jest as I figured there was dried blood on the bottom of the logs and on the ground."

"What did you decide at this point?"

"Well I knew then and there that there had been foul play. When I started putting my ducks in a row it all started to add up."

"What happened next Mr. Collis?"

"All of a sudden Francis Silver bounded into the cabin and demanded that we all leave. She screamed and swore to the top of her voice. She told us to get the hell out of her house. After parts of his remains were found outside the sheriff placed her under arrest."

"I have no other questions for Mr. Collis, Your Honor."

The judge said, "Mr. Wilson your witness."

Mr. Wilson approached Mr. Collis and asked," Mr. Collis you have told us everything you found, including ashes in the fireplace. Now…tell me who did it. Name the person that killed Mr. Silver. No, you don't know, do you?"

"No, I don't know for sure, but he had to be killed in his own house."

"No further questions Your Honor."

Judge Donnell asked lawyer Wilson if he had witnesses he would like to call.

As he replied, "Yes, Your Honor. I would like to call Mrs. Barbara Stuart to the stand.

After being sworn in and being seated he asked her to state her name for the record.

"Barbara Stuart"

"What is your relationship to the defendant?"

"Francis is my daughter."

"How did you know Charles Silver?"

"Frankie married him."

"What was your opinion of him as a person and a husband?"

"Well, on the surface he seemed like a fine young man, but the longer Frankie was married to him he seemed to change."

"Change, how do you mean?"

"Well, Frankie wouldn't complain about him but he got to where he wouldn't work and look after her and the baby. He also was drinking more and more and when he got drunk he was mean to her. He spent a lot of his time pretending to be hunting or looking for work. He was simply a loafer."

"Why do you say that?"

"Well, Frankie finally told me she had to do all the work and that he was gone a lot."

"What do you know about Charles Silver's death?"

"I don't know anything about it and was shocked to find the three of us being accused. I was just as surprised when they told me he was missing." She started sobbing.

Mr. Wilson told her, "I have no further questions."

"Mr. Alexander, your witness."

"Mrs. Stuart were you or any member of your family near the Charles Silver home on or near December twenty second?"

She stopped crying and responded. "Yes, me and my son Blackston went over to visit Frankie and take her and the baby some things I had made her for Christmas."

"Was Charles at home at this time?"

"No."

"What was Frankie doing when you arrived?"

"She was tending the baby and cleaning house. I took the baby while she finished cleaning."

"No further questions."

Several other character witnesses were called to testify on Frankie's behalf. One was Mrs. Nancy Silver who was called by Lawyer Wilson.

"Mrs. Silver how do you know the defendant, Francis Silver?"

"She is my daughter-in-law. She married my son."

"How did you get along with her?"

"I got along with her just fine. She was a hard working wife to my Charlie." Tears started flowing down her cheeks as she wiped them away. "In fact I didn't just git along with her, I loved her like a daughter. I would have done anything for her. In fact my whole family loved her."

"Your witness, Mr. Alexander."

"Mrs. Silver what do you think Francis Silver had to do with your son's death?"

"Sir...I don't want to answer that 'cause Jacob and me are having a time dealing with or understanding what has happened." She breaks down sobbing and continues wiping tears from her eyes.

"You don't have to. You may step down."

Others were called by Mr. Wilson and questioned by both lawyers. Frankie was not asked by either lawyer to take the stand in her defense. The judge asked both lawyers if they had other witnesses. They both answered that they did not. Judge Donnell then instructed them to begin their closing arguments.

"Mr. Wilson you may begin."

He stated, "I would like to remind you, the jury, that there is not sufficient evidence to convict my client, Francis Stuart Silver, of first-degree murder—period. You cannot convict her on speculation alone. She loved her husband and baby, and she could not have possibly committed such a crime against someone she loved so much. I remind you again, don't be guilty of committing a wrong yourself by finding her guilty of what you think could have happened."

The judge called on Mr. Alexander.

The prosecutor started his remarks with, "I would like to remind the jury that all evidence points to Frankie Silver. The crime took place in Charles Silver's own house. He did not have a chance to plead for his life. Gentlemen, this is a mean woman. She may not look the part, but she is vicious. Just think about what she did. What kind of woman will not only kill her man but then chop him into pieces and burn him in the fireplace? She worked so hard for days and weeks to cover up what she had done. You should without question find her guilty of first-degree murder. With or without help, she made a decision to end the life of her loving and kind husband, Charles Silver."

After the closing arguments, the judge instructed the jury to leave the courtroom to render a verdict of justice upon the defendant, Frankie Silver.

After long and arduous deliberation and consideration, the jury could not reach a decision and was kept overnight. The next day the jurors asked the judge if they could hear from some of the witnesses again; after doing so they again went into deliberation. Hours and hours passed, and the crowd was building again. Then the jurors filed into the courtroom and took their places. A hush again fell over the courtroom.

The judge asked, "Mr. Foreman has the jury reached a verdict?"

"We have, Your Honor." The foreman handed a small piece of paper to the bailiff, who in turn gave it to the judge.

"Mr. Foreman, will you please state the verdict?" the judge asked.

"We find the prisoner, Francis Stuart Silver, guilty of the felony and murder whereof she stands charged in the manner and form as charged in the bill of indictment."

Lawyer Wilson jumped to his feet. "Your Honor, I ask that a new trial be granted because the entire case is based on circumstantial evidence. It is also my understanding that the jurors were able to discuss the case during the night."

Both lawyers were called up to the bench. There was a hushed argument between them and the judge. At first the rule was granted, but after much argument from solicitor Alexander, the rule was discharged. Then the solicitor for the state asked that judgment be passed.

The judge asked Frankie to stand and face the bench for the sentencing of the court. Frankie, who had remained calm all during the trial, made her way to the front.

The judge looked her in the eyes and said, "It is the sentence of the court that the prisoner, Francis Silver, be taken to the prison from whence she came and there to remain until the next Friday of July Court of Burke County and then to be taken from thence to the place of public execution and then and there hung by the neck until she be dead. This sentence is to be carried into execution by the sheriff of Burke County."

Frankie and her lawyer made an appeal to the Supreme Court stating that the case was based on circumstantial evidence. The appeal stated that some of the witnesses had an opportunity to be together to discuss the case after the court retired.

Frankie and her attorney filed a petition to the North Carolina Supreme Court for the spring session of 1832. The records show no attorney being present to represent Frankie. The following lengthy petition was filed:

> That defendant was indicted for the murder of her husband. The case was one of circumstantial evidence. The witnesses for the state are sworn and separated under the charge of an officer until each was called into court to be examined. The case was taken to trial on Thursday morning and occupied the day in the examination of the testimony, the

argument of counsel, and the charge of the Court, the jury having retired from the bar under the charge of officers about candlelight.

The jurors were kept together in deliberation during the night and on the next day returned to the bar, and, when called over, they stated they had not yet agreed and expressed a wish to have some of the witnesses who had been examined again brought into Court that they might be satisfied about their testimony. The court directed the witness wanted to be again called in and directed the jurors to ask the questions on such points as they wished to be satisfied about.

The jurors asked the questions, and on some points the witnesses went more into detail than they had done on their first examination. The prisoner's counsel remarked that the witnesses had been separated during the trial but had been at large during the night. And the Court stated to the jurors that such was the case, that it could not have been anticipated that they would wish to hear any of the witnesses examined again after the case had been put to them and they had retired from the bar, but that the jury ought to hear the witnesses without prejudice arising from the circumstances of their having had an opportunity of being together since their former examination.

The jury ordered a verdict of guilty. The prisoner's counsel obtained a rule to show cause why a new trial should not be granted on the ground that the witnesses had been permitted to be examined by the jury on the second day when the witnesses had had an opportunity of being together after their first examination. Rule discharged and judgment of death.

The Supreme Court, after a lengthy evaluation, found there were no errors in the case. They instructed the clerk of the Superior Court of Burke County with the following:

It is considered by the Court that the judgment of the Superior Court of Law for the County of Burke be affirmed. And it is ordered that the said superior court proceed to judgment and sentence of death against the defendant, Francis Silver. On motion judgment is granted against Blackston Stuart and Isaiah Stuart, sureties to the appeal, for the cost of this court in the suit incurred.

Jno. I. Henderson, Clerk, Supreme Court of North Carolina

Frankie was taken back to her cell and stayed there until the next term of the superior court, but this was adjourned by the sheriff in the absence of the judge. This meant Frankie spent many more lonely days and nights in that small, dingy jail; in fact she was to remain in this cell for six more long months. The next term finally came, and Frankie was brought again before the bar, and the date for her execution was set again. There was much speculation and rumors by a large majority of observers that because she was a woman, she would not be executed. They expected a pardon.

The next term of the superior court was set for Friday, June 28. Frankie was again taken back to her cell, which she had occupied now for a year and two long months.

The following letter was sent to Governor Montford Stokes, who served until December 6, 1832.

Little River, 22 Sept. 1832

My Dear Governor:

On my return home from Raleigh, I was anxiously hailed and believed I had obtained a pardon for Francis Silver. On reporting that you had not yet determined whether you would pardon her or not, it seemed to strike some of your friends with considerable surprise. Since my return home, I have learned that seven persons who assigned the petition I presented to Your Excellency were seven of the jurors that convicted her. This fact was unknown to me when I had the pleasure of seeing you in Raleigh. The persons who assigned her petition who were jurors are Robert Garrison, Mr. Mackelerath, and five others whose names I do not recollect. But that seven of the names on the petition in your possession were seven of the jurors who found her guilty I feel very confident. In the source from which I received the information I have the utmost confidence. I named to Mr. Wilson, her atty, that you required further remonstrance viz. a statement from the whole of the jury that condemned her, and he, Mr. Wilson, said he would perceive and send you such petition. But whether he does or not, from this additional fact before you, I cannot help but believe your good hospitable and friendly feelings together with your good judgment will extend mercy to a humble and penitent convict. I am, my dear governor, yours in sincerity.

D. Newland

An additional note was sent from David Newland to Governor Stokes on November 3, 1832, a month before Stokes left office.

Kerner's X Roads, 3rd Nov. 1832
My Dear Governor:

You will receive in company with this a line from your son relating to the petition in favor of Mrs. Silver of Burke Co. The Stage Horn is now blowing for a start, and I am obliged to go. I can only say: pardon her if you can, and send her pardon to Theo. Wilson.

Yours in grate haste,
D. Newland

Chapter Eleven

Frankie's father knew that now was the time for him to help his daughter again. Isaiah sent Blackston down to the Morganton jail, telling him to visit with Frankie. The sheriff permitted Blackston to see her in her cell. During this first visit, he studied the lock on the door and made measurements of the keyhole in order to help his sister escape.

The lock was simple, and he thought he could make a key. He was afraid he would be caught because the deputy kept coming by to check on them. Blackston returned to the Toe River Valley and began his goal of making a key from the measurements he had made. He had been taught the art of whittling since childhood, and this was pretty easy for him. He made the key from wood, shaping it with a skill taught by his grandfather. After he finished, Isaiah and Blackston went to see Jackson Stuart, Isaiah's brother. In his little log cabin, the three made plans for Frankie's escape.

Early on the morning of May 18, the three Stuarts started another ride down to the county seat in Morganton. They rode hard and tried not to be seen by anyone. The trio stopped at a farm a few miles from Morganton. The sun was sinking to the left of the magnificent Table Rock Mountain. Isaiah talked an old farmer into selling him a wagon loaded with hay. Isaiah traded him their horses for two old workhorses. Pleased, the farmer thanked him for the unexpected trade.

The men geared up the horses and hitched them to the wagon, which they loaded with a huge amount of hay that had been included in the deal. It was getting pretty dark as the group started on the last few miles of their journey into Morganton.

It was totally dark when they arrived in town. They pulled the wagonload of hay up to the livery stable. They watered their horses and fed them some of the hay.

Meanwhile Blackston made his way to the courthouse lawn. From there he saw the only lighted room was the sheriff's office. Slipping around to the back of the courthouse, he pried open a small basement window. He slid through and into the basement. Once inside he carefully and quietly made his way upstairs and down the hall. From there he saw the light in the sheriff's office. This would not be easy because he had to go right by the open door. He stood there wondering how he would get down to where his sister was confined at the end of the hall.

He knew that Burke County had the best sheriff around, or at least he was credited with being the best, and this made Blackston's job more risky and dangerous. The new sheriff was John Boone, supposedly the grandnephew of the famed Daniel Boone. He had not been in office for very long. He had just been elected in the same election that had made Andrew Jackson president once again. A new North Carolina governor had also been chosen. Sheriff John Boone had won after a hard-fought and nasty campaign. He was the winner, but a large number resented him due to the divided nature of the campaign.

Blackston Stuart stood in the darkness of the hallway wondering how he would get to the cell. He could hear the squeak of the sheriff's chair and knew he was getting up. Blackston crouched down behind a bench located conveniently nearby. He was relieved to see the deputy sheriff walk across the dimly lit hall. The deputy stopped and stood in the spacious outside doorway looking up the street into the darkness. Blackston was glad it was the deputy instead of Sheriff Boone. The sheriff had left him in charge while he made his rounds through the town for the night.

Blackston crept down the hall with as much secrecy as possible. He was so afraid the floor might creak under his feet. Finally he made it to the cell door. He took the key from his pocket and gently slipped it into the keyhole. It went in but would not turn. He tried harder, but still it did not turn, so he reached into his pocket and pulled out another key. He slipped it into the lock and made an effort to unlock the door. At first it would not turn, so he tried harder. The key finally turned the lock. Blackston let out a long-held breath. He then slowly and carefully opened the door, hoping it would not squeak on its huge hinges.

Frankie was watching this shadowy figure lurking in the darkness and watched as he made his way into the cell. Now she knew it was her brother. She quickly threw her arms around him. They dared not speak.

The two slowly slipped up the hall and by the door. The deputy sheriff was now sitting on the front steps with his back to them. They crept down the inside stairs. Blackston helped push Frankie up until she dropped through the open window and onto the ground. He climbed through, and both were on the outside and on their way to long-awaited freedom. They headed straight toward the wagon, which was waiting nearby. As they left the courthouse lawn, they spoke their first words.

Blackston whispered, "Frankie, we'll have to hurry. We don't have long. We'll need to be very careful."

Frankie replied in a whisper, "It sure is good to see you. I knew you'd be back. I can always count on you and Dad."

In the darkness outside, they crouched along in a hurry to get to the wagon. They knew they had to rush in order to be completely out of the vicinity by sunrise. They also knew the word would spread quickly, and again they would be in danger. When they reached the wagon, Isaiah embraced Frankie and handed her some men's clothes.

He whispered softly, "Honey, put these on and crawl up in the wagon under the hay."

Frankie put them on and pushed her hair up under the broad-brimmed hat her father had given her. Then she slid into the middle of the hay. Isaiah and Blackston made sure she was fully covered. The wagon pulled out of Morganton, and Uncle Jackson followed along on his horse. The group met a man on a horse and he called loudly, "Evening. You farmers are traveling mighty late tonight, aren't you?"

Isaiah responded, "Yeah, my cows are out of hay, and we're trying to get it home to them."

This procession of make-believe farmers moved extremely slowly and seemed perfectly harmless. The sun would be coming up in a few hours. The sheriff might already be looking for them. Isaiah turned the wagon down the Rutherfordton road knowing the sheriff and his posse would be expecting them to head toward the Toe River area.

Shortly after they had left town, the sheriff returned and gave the deputy his supper. He went to the cell to check on his prisoner and give her the supper he had brought. He was shocked to find the cell empty and the door standing open.

Dropping her supper he yelled desperately to the deputy, "Oh Lord, Frankie is gone!"

The deputy came running and yelled, "No! How did this happen?"

"That's what I want to know. We'll discuss this later. Get out in the street and tell people Frankie Stuart has escaped! Alert everyone you see!"

The sheriff told him, "Ask anyone who will come armed to the courthouse, we will start a search posse."

The town was stirring hours later as the sun came up and struck the fronts of the buildings. Sheriff Boone was terribly concerned about his prisoner. His opponents had accused him of sympathizing with her anyway. He knew he had the task of finding the escaped prisoner because it was his duty as sheriff.

A little lad was holding up a newspaper and yelled, "Read all about it. The murderer Frankie Silver has escaped! Read all about it!" Before long the town was abuzz with the news.

The sheriff and his assistant had been engaged for the last few hours in planning and organizing their search. They had two possess; one would hunt close around Morganton, and the other party would head toward the Toe River area, in the direction of Frankie's home.

One of the posses finally arrived across the mountain at Kona. When Barbara Stuart was confronted about her husband and his whereabouts, she was unable to give a good answer. The word quickly spread there about Frankie's escape. Many of the settlers in the area joined the search party just as they had when Charlie had been missing. This posse had searched the main road between Morganton and Kona as they traveled up the mountain. They had been asking at all the houses if anyone had seen the escaped prisoners. The word was out, but they had not been spotted by anyone.

Several days passed. Isaiah, Blackston, Frankie, and Uncle Jackson were still traveling. They stopped and hid in the woods to rest for a while. The next day they were back on the road headed toward Rutherfordton again.

Frankie yelled, "I can't stand it here in this hay! It is too hot and itchy. Can't I just git out and walk? Is that okay with you, Dad?"

Isaiah finally agreed. "I guess it'll be all right. We're purty far out of town now anyway."

It was an extremely hot day. Frankie could not take it any longer hidden under the hay in those heavy men's clothes. It was a little past noon. She got down from the wagon to walk alongside it. She was still dressed in her overalls and oversized, floppy hat. She had her hair pushed up under the hat and stumbled along with a pitchfork across her shoulder. The hot summer sun was almost unbearable as they trudged along.

They met a man bringing a wagonload of feed home from the mill at Rutherfordton. He stopped to tell them, "Howdy, folks. It looks like you are headed to town. I've just heard from some fellows down at the mill that a murderer has escaped from the Morganton jail. She is a woman, and the law is out looking for her. If you see anything suspicious, let someone know." He bid them a good day and continued on home.

As the day progressed, Sheriff Boone and members of his posse had finished looking in the Morganton area and then split up. Some went with the sheriff in the direction of Rutherfordton. The other half went east looking for Frankie.

Soon the posse met the man taking his ground corn home, and the sheriff stopped and asked him, "Have you seen anyone suspicious while traveling up the road?"

He told them, "I have only seen four men with a wagonload of hay a mile or two back. Sheriff, I told them that a murderer had escaped and to be on the lookout for her."

Sheriff Boone thanked him and bid him a good day, and they rode on. The posse soon overtook the group of make-believe farmers. The Sheriff rode up to the group to ask if they had seen a blonde lady anywhere in the area. He described the young woman and told them why he was looking for her. He then detected a strange air of uncertainty about this odd-looking band. They were covering their faces with their hats and would not look directly at him as he talked to them.

Sheriff Boone looked at the person with the pitchfork and said with a questioning frown, "Frankie?"

Her uncle, in all his ignorance, retorted, "Her name is Tommy!"

Then Frankie, in her deepest voice, asked, "Do you want to buy some hay, mister?"

The sheriff got down from his horse, took the pitchfork, and said, "No, but we do want you, Frankie!"

The posse surrounded the group. The Stuarts did not give any resistance, and the sheriff took Frankie and her accomplices back to the prison.

Chapter Twelve

Frankie was taken along with her collaborators back to Morganton to be confined again. Her case received a lot of attention from the newspapers and the citizenry of Western North Carolina. The *Star and North Carolina Gazette* on June 7, 1833, published the following account:

> Francis Silver, who was lately convicted of murdering her husband, and sentenced to be executed on the 28th of this month, made her escape from the jail at Morganton, Burke County, on the night of the 18th ultimo by the assistance of some person or persons, who entered the jail by one of the basement story windows and opened the doors leading to the prisoners apartment by the aid of false keys. She was apprehended a few days later in Rutherford County and taken back to jail. When taken she was dressed in male apparel with her hair cut short. Her father and uncle have been committed to jail as accessories in her escape.

Frankie was still spending every hour of the day rotting away in the dark and lonely jail cell that had been her home for over a year already. She was chained to her bed. During this incarceration Sheriff Boone often talked with her and understood her torment and sorrow. There were times when he had to go to her cell because she was screaming in her sleep. Often he found her sobbing openly on her cot. Sheriff Boone was truly a caring person and was exceptionally nice to

Frankie. He carried her meals to her there in the courthouse jail and often talked with her while she was eating.

He dreaded the time that he might be required to carry out her hanging. He realized and hoped there might be a stay of execution due to the fact that no woman had ever been hanged in North Carolina. The death sentence was postponed once again. The sheriff was elated. He hoped this was a sign that he would not have to be in charge of putting her to death.

The new date of her execution was July 12, 1833. The sheriff was convinced it would again be postponed, and he knew there had been many letters sent to Governor David L. Swain begging him to pardon the prisoner. Lawyer Wilson submitted the following letter on Frankie's behalf:

Morganton, June 12, 1833

Dear Sir:

Yours of the 3rd of May was rec'd on the 5th of this instant by the Buncombe mail. It will be treated as confidential & private. I have showed it to no one except the father of the unfortunate wretch who was the subject of your letter, & that in order to put him on his guard that he need not trust too much to others, & he having too that he would inform her of her imminent danger.

I have never been satisfied with the case made for the Supreme Court by His Honor Judge Donnell. The witness, after the jury had retired & had been out for the space of twenty-four hours, were permitted (by the Court) to undergo a reexamination by the jury & that too on the very subject & ground taken for her defense & which before had not been touched on by them. I still believe that if the case had been fairly presented to the Supreme Court, she would have had the advantage of a new trial. Still it might not in the end have availed her anything.

You will have perceived that she effected her escape on the Monday night after superior court, but owing to the great flood that happened at that very time, she was unable to elude the [illegible words] of his prisoner who brought her on the 8th day after her escape. On her return to jail, she became hopeless, sent for some of her acquaintances, & made a confession of the whole facts as the accused (as is believed by many) from the circumstances of the case. Both Herman Gaither and I were asked then to sign a petition for her, but we proposed to see her ourselves. We went to the jail, and I beg leave to remark S. Hilman was at the time perfectly taken & at himself from a rigid examination & cross-examination. We were all of the opinion that it was clearly a case of manslaughter if not justifiable homicide. This was always my opinion from the circumstances proved and the facts attending the case. I am confident if the facts could have been proved as they really were, it would have amounted to no more than manslaughter. I am satisfied too that she could have had no idea of her confession being made use of as a case of the kind mentioned.

There are three persons bound over for aiding in her escape. I do not believe they can be convicted without her testimony. She has informed me of the persons, & it may be more important to public justice that they should be made examples of rather than her. A petition will be forwarded in a few days praying for executive clemency with many respectable assignors to cause. Old Mr. Rutherford & others. I declare to you that, as her lawyer who defended her, I have no feelings on the subject; they are only such as every man must have at the idea of such a shaking light as it must be to every man or human being possessed of the feelings of humanity. I do sincerely believe it is the wish & desire of the better of the community that she may be pardoned.

I do believe, though, that there are some like the woman who went home crying a pardon had been granted to a poor culprit & she had missed seeing a great sight. It cannot be necessary that for public example a poor wretch should be executed of her appearance & she too a female.

It is now 18 months that she has undergone confinement, a great part of the time chained in a dungeon to the middle of the room. It is possible that her case is only a case of manslaughter. It was argued by many, the solicitor too, that she must have killed him (Charles Silver) while he was lying asleep by the fire, which was surely possible. He went from his father near dark, perfectly cool & sober, in the dead of winter, the house very open.

I say it is not probable that he would have lain down to sleep by the fire. She must have killed him with some unlikely blow not premeditated. Please to accept my best wishes for yourself and family.

Th. W. Wilson

Another letter was sent accompanying a petition from a group of ladies.

To His Excellency David L. Swain
Morganton, June 30th 1833

Governor of the State of N. C.:

You will be somewhat surprised at seeing this petition and letter after our making on your part a peremptory refusal to pardon without a different [illegible word] on the [illegible word] of the affair could be produced. Mr. Stuart, the father of the prisoner, was advised by Col. John Carson as being a means by which he might possibly obtain a pardon together with others of the village to get up a petition among the ladies. The prisoner, however, knows nothing of it but is preparing for death; to this proceeding, however, I have not advised either of or against. Though the minds of the people seem to be very much softened in her behalf since the determination on your behalf with regard to a pardon. I am requested by Mr. Stuart to ask Your Excellency to add an addition to her respite. He thinks he will be able to add new light on the subject, and the people think if there is any ground upon which to add to time, it might be possible to aid in the cause of justice and humanity.

Respectfully,
Your Obedient. Servant.
WC Bevins

The following petition was sent to the governor:

Petition to Gov. David L. Swain from the ladies of Burke and Buncombe counties

June 29, 1833

To His Excellency David L. Swain, Governor of the State of North Carolina:

Your petitioners are fully sensible of the delicacy of presenting to you this petition. Yet they justify themselves by claiming as a duty peculiar to the life to be always on the side of mercy toward their fellow beings and to the female more particularly.

The subject of this petition is an unfortunate creature of our sex, Mrs. Frances Silver, who was sentenced by our court to be executed on the last Friday in June but, by your goodness, was respited until the second Friday in July. We do not expect to refer you to any information in this that you are not already familiarly acquainted with unless it be the treatment the unfortunate creature received during the life of her husband.

We do not refer you to this with a view of justification but merely to reiterate the various unfortunate events that have taken place in the world in consequence of ill-grounded abuse, indecorous and insupportable treatment in which the creature now before Your Excellency for mercy has, contrary to the laws of God & and the country yet so consistent with our nature, been her own avenger.

The husband of the unfortunate creature now before you, we are informed, sir, was one of that cast of mankind who are wholly dissolute of any of the feeling that is necessary to make a good Husband or parent—the neighborhood people are convinced that his treatment to her was both unbecoming and cruel very often and at the time too when female delicacy would most forbid it. He treated her with personal violence. He was said by all the neighborhood to have been a man who never made use of any exertions to support either his wife or child, which terminated, as frequently is the case that those duties nature ordered and intended the husband to perform were thrown to her. His own relatives admit of his having been a lazy, trifling man. It is also admitted by them that she was an industrious woman. But for the want of grace, religion, and refinement, she has committed an act that she herself would have given a world to have been able to call back. We refer you to her child, who is an infant and needs the protection of a mother. We hope that Your Excellency will extend to the unfortunate female all the mercy you can.

> Even to pardon & wipe from the character of the
> female in this community the stigma of a woman
> being hung under the gallows.

This petition had thirty-three signatures of ladies from Morganton and Buncombe County, North Carolina. A large part of the general public fully anticipated a pardon due to the number of petitions and the prestige of the signers.

Sheriff Boone waited patiently for the news of a pardon, but he, like Frankie, was gradually losing hope. The execution date was drawing closer each day.

It was his role as sheriff to have a scaffold built for the execution. He reluctantly asked the carpenters to go ahead and build the gallows, hoping they would never be used. They built it on a hill close to town. The sheriff continued to wait patiently for a stay of execution from the governor, but none came.

Early on the morning of July 12, 1833, store owners opened their businesses and began to get ready for a normal day of trade. But it was already anything but a typical day. Before long, hordes of people ascended on the little town of Morganton. They wanted to attend the first execution of a woman in North Carolina. The papers had kept everyone informed on the matter of the woman who had chopped her husband up and disposed of him in the fireplace. Her subsequent escape and capture had also added to the notoriety of the matter. There were those who secretly sympathized with her and those who despised her for her dastardly deed.

The sheriff took Frankie her breakfast and talked with her briefly, explaining that no word had come to stop her execution. Tears welled up in his eyes as he told her he would come for her at two o'clock to take her to the place of hanging.

Frankie told him, "I appreciate all your kindnesses, sir. I have no hard feelings for you."

He did not let her see him weep as he returned to his office. He felt the punishment was much too harsh. He thought if she'd had a better lawyer, he would have told her to claim self-defense. He had a daughter near the same age, and this might have been the reason for some of his deep concern and sympathy for Frankie.

Sheriff Boone came to her cell and asked if she would like a visit from the preacher.

"Yes, you can bring him in. I will be glad to see him.

The sheriff left to get Preacher Thomas. Before long he appeared again with preacher Thomas. He let him in the cell. How are you, Preacher Thomas? I'm glad you care enough to come see me. I don't deserve your time."

"How are you holding up, Frankie?"

"I'm so tired of this jail. I'm going crazy."

"The folks at the church are praying for you.

Is there anything I can do for you before you leave?"

"No, I don't know of anything. When you see Mom, Dad, and Blackston, tell them I love them."

"I certainly will the next time I see them. Frankie, are you ready to meet your maker? I remember when you asked Christ to be your Savior. Have you asked forgiveness for all your sins?"

"Yes, as best I can, but I don't seem to get an answer to my prayers. They don't seem to go above the ceiling of this stinking jail. I don't believe God can forgive such an awful thing."

"No, Frankie, you are wrong. God forgives us of all our sins. Sometimes we think it is just some that He forgives, but the Bible tells us He forgives us all our sins. Do you mind if we have a word of prayer before I leave?"

"No, that will be fine, Preacher."

"Let's bow now and talk to the Lord. Dear God and heavenly Father, hallowed be thy name. I come to you today thanking you for your grace and forgiveness of our sins. I come to you today on behalf of Frankie and ask that you be with her today and forgive her for all her trespasses. You tell us that you forgive us for all our sins—not just some but all our sins. Please, Lord, comfort and be with both families in this trying hour. Lord, I pray you will help those who harbor ill will. May they surrender that hate and turn their hearts over to you. Bless Frankie in this hour if it be your will. In Jesus's name I pray. Amen."

The preacher hugged Frankie and told her good-bye and that he would be praying for her and her baby.

That afternoon Frankie was taken from her nasty jail cell by the sheriff and his deputies and helped into a wagon. The somber procession started on its way through a crowd of people yelling and screaming at her. She rode in the back of the wagon with armed deputies on each side. The sheriff followed on his horse. Frankie held her head high. This infuriated the crowd. She did not shed a tear, and she looked straight into the crowd.

At that point the mass of people was almost totally out of hand. Many were inebriated and yelling, although some were quiet and somber.

Ellie Maude and Eliza Burgner were in this boisterous crowd and, as usual, had plenty to say.

"Eliza, I knew you'd be here," said Ellie Maude. "Have you ever seen such a crowd? I just don't believe this is actually happening. You remember what you said? I guess you are wrong this time."

"Well, Ellie, I'm certainly not wrong very often. I knew you'd be here to rub it in. Let's just say it ain't happened yet. That's why I came. I didn't actually want to see this horrible thing, but I still don't think it's going to happen. The governor may still pardon her in the last minute. I understand there have been many letters sent to Governor Swain to pardon her. My signature is on one of them. I keep looking for someone to come flying in here on a horse with word from the governor."

"There's no talk of a pardon here in town. 'Sides, there's no need to git riled. She has been in that jail cell now for over a year. I'm gittin' plumb put out with them. I think it's time they either set her free or follow through with the judge's orders. Now, don't you dare tell anyone where you heard what I'm a fixin to tell you. I told you before, and I'm telling you again, I think Sheriff Boone is too involved with his prisoner. I certainly don't think he would be that caring if this were a man in his jail, do you? I'm not sayin' they are doing anything wrong. You know what I mean. But he is pow'ful good to her."

"I agree with you, Ellie, but he may still believe, as I do, that this poor girl did it in self-defense. He might just be concerned because she is a woman. I certainly don't see anything wrong with being nice to her."

"Hush yourself up, Eliza. I see them coming! Lord have mercy, they are really bringing her in that wagon."

"I can't believe this is finally happening."

"We may actually see the end of this today!"

The group moved slowly, and the mob grew larger as they went along. When they reached the hill where the scaffold was located, it was almost impossible to get through the large throng. Many of them followed until Frankie reached the place of execution. The deputies helped open up a way for the wagon to go through to the gallows. Once the wagon arrived, Sheriff Boone and his men helped Frankie out.

At that point the mass of people was almost totally out of hand. Many were inebriated and yelling, although some were quiet and somber.

The somber, slow-moving group made its way through the large crowd and to the gallows. They almost had to fight to get through the yelling screaming mob.

The sheriff stepped up on the steps to the scaffold and yelled to the crowd, "You all need to calm down! We can't proceed with this kind of disruption." He stepped back down, took Frankie by the arm, and started toward the gallows. Someone in the crowd ran out to Frankie and handed her a piece of strawberry cake. Frankie took it and told her how much she appreciated it. One of the deputies handed the sheriff a black hood for Frankie. The sheriff and Frankie made their way up the steps as she ate the cake. The jeering and yelling began again.

When they reached the top, the sheriff raised his hands to quiet the crowd. He asked Frankie, "Do you have anything you would like to say?"

Her father, who was standing far back from the crowd with Barbara and Blackston, yelled with a thunderous voice, "Die with it in you, Frankie!"

She asked the sheriff if he would remove her handcuffs for just a moment. The people gasped as he did as she requested.

"Ellie Maude, can you believe this?" Eliza asked. "He has taken her handcuffs off."

"It only confirms what I've been telling you all along. He would not have done this for a man. I'm sure he treats her special now."

"Look, she's gettin something from inside her dress!"

Frankie reached into her bosom, took out a piece of crumpled paper, and began to read:

This dreadful, dark, and dismal day
Has swept my glories all away.

My sun goes down, my days are past
And I must leave this world at last.

Oh Lord, what will become of me?
I am condemned you all now see.
To heaven or hell my soul must fly
All in a moment when I die.

Judge Donnell has my sentence passed
The prison walls I leave at last.
Nothing to cheer my drooping head
Until I am numbered with the dead.

But oh! That dreadful Judge I fear
Shall I that awful sentence hear?
"Depart ye cursed down to hell
And forever there to dwell."

I know that frightful ghost I'll see
Gnawing flesh in misery
And then and there attended be
For murder in the first degree.

There shall I meet that mournful face
Whose blood I spilled upon this place
With flaming eyes to me he'll say
"Why did you take my life away?"

His feeble hands fell gently down
His chattering tongue soon lost its sound

To see his soul and body part
It strikes with terror to my heart.

I took his blooming days away
Left him no time to God to pray
And sins fall on his head
Must I not bear them in his stead?

The jealous thought that first gave strife
To make me take my husband's life.
For months and days I spent my time
Thinking how to commit this crime.

And on a dark and doleful night
I put his body out of sight.
With flames I tried him to consume
But time would not admit it done.

You all see me and on me gaze.
Be careful how you spend your days
And never commit this awful crime
But try to serve your God in time.

My mind on solemn subjects rolls
My little child. God bless its soul!
All you who are of Adam's race
Let not my faults this child disgrace.

Farewell good people, you all now see
What my bad conduct's brought me:
To die of shame and of disgrace
Before this world of human race.

Awful indeed to think of death
In perfect health to lose my breath.
Farewell, my friends, I bid adieu
Vengeance on me must now pursue.

Great God! How shall I be forgiven?
Not fit for earth, not fit for heaven
But little time to pray to God.
For now I try that awful road.

A deadly hush had fallen over the huge throng. Many were sobbing and wiping tears from their eyes. Frankie slowly tucked the poem inside her dress. She looked to the sheriff and then gave him a nod. He walked over and gently replaced her handcuffs.

The sheriff tried to control his emotions as he placed the hood over her head and then the heavy noose. Many in the audience were praying out loud. Some just folded their hands and prayed silently. Some people dropped to their knees and loudly asked for God's intervention. Then someone could be heard saying, "Where is the pardon? Where is the pardon?"

The sheriff stepped down from the scaffold and went to the back. There he gave the executioner, a stranger from Raleigh, the signal to release the trap door. The crowd gasped, and children were crying as Frankie struggled for a brief moment and then grew completely still. Everyone was completely motionless for what seemed like an eternity.

The crowd began slowly to disperse, some in sadness and some with an unspoken satisfaction. It was a moment that would stay with them all for the rest of their lives. The last to remain were Frankie's mother, father, and brother, who had been watching from a distance. They waited patiently for everyone to leave.

And then they slowly made their way, trying not to be observed, toward the gallows. Isaiah and Blackston were holding Barbara as she wept bitterly.

Chapter Thirteen

Sheriff John Boone instructed the deputies with a weak and trembling voice, "Lift her body, and close the trap door. Please, lower her body gently. Get the hood and noose off her. Please, let her down respectfully."

Sheriff Boone and the deputies let Frankie's family see her for the last time. They said their final good-byes. Barbara screamed and collapsed across the body. Isaiah and Blackston were on their knees holding on to Barbara.

Sheriff Boone told them, "Take your time. We are not in a hurry."

They stayed for several minutes, and then the three of them left Frankie's remains completely heartbroken.

Another wagon arrived, driven by the undertaker. In this wagon was a wooden slatted coffin. The sheriff and his two deputies helped the undertaker removed it from the wagon and carry it up onto the scaffold. The four men gently placed the body of Frankie Silver into the crude handmade coffin. The men loaded it in the undertaker's wagon.

The sheriff told the undertaker, "Please, take her to the train station." He shook his head and said, "The powers that be in Raleigh have asked me to send the body to Chapel Hill. They need it at the medical school. I understand they never get a female body to examine. Tell the attendant at the station I will be there later to give him all his shipping instructions. It seems cruel to me that the family can't claim the body, but I am not the judge. I just do what the judge orders."

The sun was setting in the west as Sheriff Boone and the others returned to the courthouse. The sheriff made his evening rounds through town. It took longer than usual because he had to stop and talk to everyone who wanted to confront him about the hanging. He finally went by the train station to give the clerk the information. He told the clerk where to send the body. When the sheriff arrived, the coffin was sitting outside on a rail cart. The sky was almost dark, and the July heat was sweltering. He inquired about what time the train would arrive and then gave the clerk the rest of the information he needed to deliver this unique shipment. The sheriff told him it was to be sent to a Chapel Hill medical facility for students to use for dissection.

He left the clerk and continued on his evening patrol. The clerk wrote out the delivery instructions that were to be placed on the coffin. He went out back of the depot to use the outhouse. He then got some packages that were also to be picked up by the incoming train. He was only gone for ten or fifteen minutes.

He returned to his post near the window, where he could see the tracks. He put the packages down near the door. He pulled out his gold pocket watch to check the time. He knew it was about time for the train traveling east to arrive, so he picked up the packages and went outside with instructions for the conductor. He could hear the distant whistle and rumble of the train coming down the tracks as it rolled into Morganton.

When he approached the cart, he was utterly shocked to find the coffin missing. He rushed to look all around the building and inside. The coffin was nowhere to be found. He first thought it might be a prank by some of the boisterous crowd from earlier.

The train had come to a steaming halt and was now waiting on the tracks for the clerk. He gave the conductor the other packages and then had to tell him to go on without the corpse.

The clerk ran down the street and found a man to go tell the sheriff, and let him know the body had been stolen. It was a good while before the sheriff was found and informed about what was going on.

Meanwhile Isaiah, Blackston, and Barbara were on their way with the stolen coffin toward their Toe River home. They had not been spotted by anyone yet. They had a hard time traveling in the total darkness. Occasionally the moon came out from behind the clouds and helped light their way, but they dared not use a light.

The extreme heat of the summer night made matters worse. The trio knew they would have a stinking corpse on their hands before long. They soon realized there was no way they could make it all the way across the mountain without being caught. Struggling with their grief and sorrow, all three trudged along. They knew they would soon be followed.

Blackston kept saying, "What are we going to do? Dad, what are we going to do?"

They had traveled a good distance out of town. The somber procession finally arrived at the Buckhorn Tavern about eight miles from Morganton, and there they stopped, rested, and sent Blackston inside to get something to eat and drink. The stage had stopped there before dark and the place was full of people who were spending the night.

After getting the food and water Blackston asked the proprietor, "We need to borrow a shovel for a couple of hours. We have spilt a couple of sacks of corn in our wagon that we are taking to the mill and need to shovel it up and put it back into the sacks. We will bring it back in an hour or so."

The proprietor told him, "You folks sure are traveling late aren't you? Look outside in the shed there's one out there. Do you have a lantern?"

Blackston replied, "Yes, thank you. We have one in the wagon."

They took the wagon on up the old road and stopped a short distance above the tavern. They started digging a grave there beside the road. Isaiah held the lantern while Blackston dug, then Isaiah dug awhile as Blackston held the lantern. The digging got very difficult at times due to the tree roots.

Meanwhile a little girl who lived with her family at the tavern was playing outside, throwing rocks and watching bats chase them. She was getting ready to go inside because of the darkness. She was about ten years old with braided blonde pigtails. She stopped in her tracks at what she saw. There was an eerie glow coming from the edge of the woods. She stopped a moment and decided to go see where the light was coming from. She slipped behind a tree and saw the place where the grave was being dug. She did this without being seen.

She continued to watch as the Stuarts put the coffin in the ground and began to cover it. Barbara was wailing violently. This scared the little girl so badly she ran back toward the tavern as fast as her feet would carry her. She was so glad these people had not seen her. Out of breath, she slipped back down the hill to safety. She was afraid to tell anyone what she had seen.

Barbara, Blackston, and Isaiah finally left the unmarked grave there on the edge of the pine woods. Blackston returned the shovel, and they started on their way to Kona. When they reached the Toe River Valley, they went to their church cemetery. There they worked far into the night to dig some fresh, shallow graves in the darkness. They returned home and waited, knowing the sheriff would come.

The sheriff was grief stricken and tired from the long day. He decided it was not necessary to look for the body until he'd had some rest and something to eat. He waited until the next day. He and some of his men went to ask the Stuarts if they had stolen the corpse. They, of course, denied having anything to do with the matter.

Isaiah told him, "We'd appreciate it if you would leave us alone. Our daughter is dead. Ain't that enough, Mr. Sheriff?"

The sheriff and his men found the unmarked graves and tried to exhume the stolen coffin. They dug a few feet in the fresh dirt and hit ground that had not been disturbed. They realized that Frankie's folks had done this trying to fool them.

The sheriff knew it was the Stuarts who had stolen the body, but he decided not to pursue the matter any further even if it meant that the place of her burial would never be known to anyone except the family. Inside he understood the agony the Stuarts were going through.

A little bit later Mr. Bevins received this letter from Governor
David Swain:

July 9, 1833

Dear Sir:

I have received your letter without date but post-
marked on the 3rd inst. Together with the accompanying petition of a number of the most
respectable ladies of your vicinity on behalf of the
unfortunate Mrs. Silver, who, before this communication can reach you, will in all human probabil-
ity have passed the boundary that separates us alike
from the reproaches of enemies and the sympathies
of friends. All that it is now in my power to do is
unite, in the anxious wish that doubtless pervades
the whole community to which she belongs, that
she may find that mercy in heaven that seemed to
be necessarily denied upon earth, a free pardon for
all the offenses in her life.
I beg you to assure the fair petitioners, the most of
whom I have the pleasure of acquaintances with,
that the benevolent motives that influenced their
memorial on behalf of the unfortunate convict are
duly appreciated and that no one can participate
more deeply than I do in their sympathy for her
melancholy fate.

I am, sir, very respectfully your obedient servant.

D. L. Swain

This letter was read with disdain by the ladies who signed the petition and many more throughout the community. They believed that Governor Swain had purposefully avoided a very difficult decision because the letter was clearly dated June 30, 1833. The ladies felt he was trying to say he did not get the letter in time to save her from execution.

We will never know all the facts of this story, for they followed the characters to an untimely grave. Could this tragedy possibly have had a different ending? Love is like a garden—it must be cultivated to keep it alive. In the beginning there was much love and respect in this young couple, but it was choked out by neglect. A lack of communication and failure to resolve differences lead to this awful end. What a terrible price they all paid.

The Bible says the sins of one generation are visited upon the next. That has proven to be true in this case.

There was one more court entry for the victims of this tragedy, dated April 1836. It was perhaps the saddest one of them all. It read:

> Ordered by the court that Nancy Silver, an orphan daughter of Francis Silver, deceased, being about five years old on the 3rd day of November 1835, be bound unto Barbara Stuart until she is eighteen years of age; to receive at her freedom one cow and calf, two suits of clothes, one good bed and furniture, and twelve months' schooling.

Sometime later the little girl who had observed the late-night burial heard her relatives talking about the hanging in Morganton and how the body had been stolen. She then told them what she had witnessed. They went to the spot in the pine woods just above the tavern. There they found an unmarked grave where the little girl said she had witnessed the scary burial that night by lantern light.

The Unmarked Grave

Appendix

THIS PHOTO IS OF FRANKIE'S HEADSTONE TAKEN IN 1966, IT
READS: "FRANKIE SILVERS ONLY WOMAN EVER HANGED IN
BURKE COUNTY, HANGING, MORGANTON: JULY 12, 1833."

The spelling should be "Silver," without the S. the statement that
she was the only woman ever hanged is disputed. There are some ac-
counts of a woman slave who was hanged. I found in my research that
Francis was spelled Frances in places and Stuart was spelled Stewart
in many places. I have used consistent spelling of these names except
in the official documents.

This stone is in an overgrown pine thicket and was very hard to
locate. In 1952 a Morganton newspaper, *The News Herald*, and some
friends and subscribers of the paper placed this marker after the grave
had been unmarked for more than a hundred years. It is ten or fifteen

feet from the bank of a very old roadbed. To me it seemed so dark, lonesome, and dreary there in the woods.

ANOTHER PICTURE TAKEN ON AUGUST 21, 2013 OF THE SAME MARKER:

Haskell A. Davis

THIS PICTURE IS OF THE REMAINS OF AN OLD BUILDING ON THE JAKE DUVAULT PLACE POSSIBLY THE BUCKHORN TAVERN, TAKEN IN 1966. IT MAY NOT BE THE TAVERN BUT I BELIEVE IT IS NEAR WHERE THE BUCKHORN TAVERN WOULD HAVE BEEN. THIS WAS LOCATED JUST BELOW WHERE FRANKIE WAS BURIED.

THIS IS AN OLD WELL SHED LOCATED NEAR THE OLD BUILD-
ING AND BURIAL SITE. THIS PICTURE WAS TAKEN IN 1966.

THIS IS THE OLD HOUSE WHERE CHARLIE SILVER GREW UP. IT IS WELL OVER
TWO HUNDRED YEARS OLD. THE HOUSE HAS BEEN REMODELED AND
REWORKED MANY TIMES. IT IS A MIRACLE IT IS STILL STANDING TODAY.

THE TALL, WHITE STONE MARKS THE RESTING PLACE OF
CHARLIE'S GRANDFATHER, GEORGE SILVER, JR.

THIS IS KONA BAPTIST CHURCH TODAY. THIS PICTURE WAS
TAKEN IN JUNE 2013. INSIDE THIS CHURCH IS WHERE THE
MUSEUM FOR FRANKIE AND CHARLIE IS LOCATED.

THIS IS A PICTURE OF THE SILVER HOME AND THE
CHURCH ON THE HILL IN THE BACKGROUND.

THE THREE STONES IN THE FOREGROUND ARE MARKERS
FOR THE REMAINS OF CHARLIE SILVER.

REVEREND JACOB SILVER, FATHER OF CHARLIE. HE SERVED A
NUMBER OF CHURCHES INCLUDING GREEN MOUNTAIN,
DOUBLE ISLAND, AND BIG IVY BAPTIST.

THIS IS THE HEAD STONE OF ALFRED SILVER BROTHER TO CHARLES
SILVER. HE WAS BORN NOVEMBER 15, 1816 AND DIED SEPTEMBER 10, 1905.
HE IS BURIED IN THE OLD SILVER CEMETERY ON CURTISS CREEK IN OLD
FORT, NORTH CAROLINA. THE BEST ACCOUNT OF THIS ENTIRE SAGA
WAS TOLD BY ALFRED IN A 1900 INTERVIEW BY "RED BUCK" BRYANT
WHO OFTEN WROTE FOR THE NEWS-HERALD IN MORGANTON.

THIS IS THE GRAVE MARKER OF REV. JACOB SILVER
FATHER OF CHARLES, 1791–1887.

THIS IS A PICTURE OF SHERIFF JOHN BOONE'S GRAVE MARKER. IT HAS BEEN BROKEN, AND SOMEONE HAS GLUED IT BACK TOGETHER. THIS PICTURE WAS TAKEN IN 2000. I VISITED IT AGAIN RECENTLY AND NOW THIS CEMETERY IS COMPLETELY GROWN OVER WITH WEEDS AND BUSHES.

Sheriff John ("Esquire") Boone's grave is located between Morganton and Lenoir, North Carolina. He served two terms as High Sheriff of Burke County. His first term was 1832–33 and the second was 1836–37. He had to let one term lapse due to state law before he could serve his second term in 1836–37. He died in office during his second term on November 22, 1837. He and his wife, Isabella, are buried in the old Kincaid Cemetery. His father, Johnathan Boone, and his mother, Susannah, are also buried there.

In an interview with a distant relative of Sheriff John Boone, I was told his grandfather had told him about the concern and broken heart the sheriff had over the execution of Frankie Silver. Thanks to all who continue to keep this story alive and have done something to help preserve some of this history.

Bibliography

Sharpe, Bill. *A New Geography*, Vols. I and II. Raleigh, NC: Sharpe Publishing Company, 1958.

Arthur, John Preston. *Western North Carolina, A History from 1730 to 1913*. Asheville, NC, Edward and Broughton Printing Company, 1914.

Hunter, Elizabeth. "Remarkable History of the Silvers Family." *Mitchell Journal* (July 24, 1980).

Avery, Clifton K. "The Official Court Record of the Trial, Conviction and Execution of Frankie Silver." *News-Herald*, 1953.

Hiergesell, Geneva. "Family Interpretation of Murder." *Morganton News-Herald*, March 28, 1968.

Lloyd Richard Bailey, Sr., Editor, *The Heritage of the Toe River Valley, Vol. I* Walsworth Publishing Company, Inc., Marceline, Mo. 64658 (1994), 66–72.

All Scripture quotations are taken from the King James Version of the Holy Bible

www.ingramcontent.com/pod-product-compliance
Lightning Source LLC
Chambersburg PA
CBHW061208170626
46809CB00003B/1285